# JUNIOR

# CLASSICS

Published in Red Turtle by
Rupa Publications India Pvt. Ltd 2016
7/16, Ansari Road, Daryaganj
New Delhi 110002

*Sales centres:*
Allahabad Bengaluru Chennai
Hyderabad Jaipur Kathmandu
Kolkata Mumbai



ISBN: 978-81-291-3895-8

Second impression 2017

10 9 8 7 6 5 4 3 2

Printed at Rakmo Press Pvt. Ltd, New Delhi

# Contents

Sense
and
Sensibility
Jane Austen

The Dashwood family had been living in Sussex for a long time. They stayed at Norland Park, at the heart of their property, and had a good reputation among their acquaintances.

The owner of this vast estate was unmarried, and so had invited his nephew, a Mr Henry Dashwood, and his family to live with him at Norland Park.

The old gentleman spent his last days in comfort, aided by his relatives.

Mr Henry Dashwood had a son, John, by a previous marriage, and three daughters—Elinor, Marianne and Margaret—by his second wife. John Dashwood was a respectable man, made rich by the fortune he inherited from his mother. His own marriage increased his wealth.

Therefore, Norland was not as important to John as it was to his half-sisters. Their mother owned nothing and their father had only 10,000 pounds of his own.

When Henry's uncle died, however, his will revealed that John and John's four-year-old Harry would inherit his entire estate.

So, John's father Henry was left with only the 10,000 pounds. His disappointment was severe but he was cheerful by nature and felt that he and his family could manage if they lived within their means.

However, Henry died about a year after his uncle, leaving Mrs Dashwood and her daughters with no permanent home of their own, and with just 10,000 pounds.

John was generally well-respected and conducted himself properly while doing his normal duties. However, his wife, Fanny Dashwood, was a caricature of her husband—she was selfish and narrow-minded.

John had promised his father that he would help his half-sisters financially; and was planning to give each of them 1,000 pounds. However, his wife convinced him that 500 would be enough.

Fanny Dashwood did not get along with her husband's family, and made it difficult for them to live after Henry Dashwood's death. Mrs Dashwood would have left the house immediately but for the entreaties of her eldest daughter, and her love for all her three daughters. Still, she made numerous enquiries about a suitable house in the area, and got no response.

Elinor, the eldest of Mrs Dashwood's daughters, possessed strength of character and coolness of judgment even though she was just nineteen. Sixteen-year-old Marianne was as romantic as Elinor was sensible. And the youngest, Margaret, was a well-disposed and good-humoured girl. At thirteen, she had already absorbed Marianne's romantic nature though she lacked Marianne's sense and could not see herself as equal to her sisters who were at a more advanced stage of life.

In the meanwhile, Elinor was forming an attachment with Edward Ferrars, Fanny's brother who had been visiting them. Although Edward was not very handsome or charming, he was a shy, pleasant gentleman. He was also a rich man's eldest son; however, since his father had passed away, Edward's fortune depended on the will of his mother.

Mrs Dashwood approved of Edward, but Elinor felt her mother would like him even more as she got to know him better.

Mrs Dashwood said that as soon as she saw a sign of Edward's love for Elinor, and thought that a serious friendship was certain, she would happily organize the wedding.

'Marianne,' she said to her second daughter, in all probability, Elinor will soon be married. We'll miss her but she will be happy.'

***

But Fanny Dashwood could not help playing spoilsport. She pointed out, rather cruelly, that her mother would only allow her two sons marry wealthy girls.

Mrs Dashwood answered her contemptuously, but decided that Elinor shouldn't be exposed to such behaviour even for another week.

So, when a letter arrived from a relative of hers, Sir John Middleton, offering on easy terms a small cottage far away from Norland, she accepted immediately.

***

Mrs Dashwood got great pleasure in telling Fanny and John that she would be leaving with her daughters soon.

She very kindly invited Fanny and John to visit her. She also extended an invitation to Edward—very affectionately.

John apologized, saying that since the cottage was so far from Norland, he would be unable to help in sending his mother's considerable furniture, which would be sent by water.

They shed many tears as they left Norland and were dejected in the initial part of their journey, especially since Edward's farewell to Elinor had been very stiff. But as their journey drew to its end, they began to take interest in the countryside which would soon be their home. Barton Valley gave them a feeling of cheerfulness. It was pleasant, wooded and fertile.

Barton Cottage was small, compact and comfortable, and had a good location—high hills ascended right behind it. Barton village was mainly on one of the hills and afforded a pleasing view from the windows of the cottage.

***

Sir John and Lady Middleton lived in great style in the huge and handsome Barton Park. They always had guests, and Sir John often went hunting and shooting and his wife took care of the children.

When Mrs Dashwood and her children visited, Sir John welcomed them at the door. They would meet, he said, one other gentleman at that time, besides Lady Middleton's mother, Mrs Jennings, a fat, witty person.

The gentleman in question was Colonel Brandon, Sir John's friend, a silent and serious man. He had a pleasing appearance. However, Margaret

and Marianne felt he was a complete, old bachelor, for he was more than thirty-five years old.

It was Mrs Jennings who pronounced one day that Colonel Brandon was in love with Marianne Dashwood. She suspected this when Marianne sang for them on the first evening. She was convinced it would be a great match: she was lovely and he was rich.

Marianne told her mother that the Colonel was far too old and ill to fall in love. Elinor defended him, but added that his rheumatism could be a problem.

When Elinor left the room, Marianne turned to her mother. She was worried about Edward Ferrars.

'I'm sure he's not well. It's been a fortnight and he hasn't showed up here. What else could have kept him at Norland?' she asked.

***

One day, Marianne and Margaret were out walking, when clouds sent driving rain on their faces.

Marianne missed a step and slipped on the ground. Just then, a gentleman—with two pointer dogs and a gun—came by. He laid down his gun and rushed to assist her. Her foot was twisted and she could barely stand. The gentleman carried her in his arms down the hill. He took her straight into the cottage and seated her in a chair.

Elinor and Mrs Dashwood were amazed by the scene before them. The handsome stranger explained everything in a graceful and frank manner that won appreciation from Mrs Dashwood.

She thanked the man repeatedly and invited him take a seat. But he declined since he was wet and dirty. He introduced himself as Willoughby and said that he lived at Allenham and would call the next day to enquire about Miss Dashwood.

His good looks and grace were discussed in great detail. Marianne too joined in the admiration though she had not really seen him very clearly because of her injury.

When Sir John heard that Willoughby was in the country, he said, 'This is good news. I will ride to his place and invite him for dinner on Thursday.'

'What kind of man is he?' Mrs Dashwood asked.

'He's a good fellow. A decent shot and a bold rider!'

But Marianne was indignant.

'What are his habits, genius and his talents?'

A puzzled Sir John answered, 'I don't know that much about him.'

'Who is he?' asked Elinor, 'and from where does he come?'

Sir John did not know. He said he had no property there but visited the old woman to whom he was related at Allenham Court.

***

Willoughby visited the next morning and enquired about the injured lady. Marianne received him with more than mere politeness.

'Marianne,' said Elinor, as soon as Willoughby had left, 'for one morning I think you have done pretty well. You even know what the gentleman thinks about Alexander Pope! Soon you will have exhausted every preferred topic. Another meeting and you'll have nothing more to ask!'

'Elinor,' said Marianne, 'is this fair? But I see what you mean. I have been open and sincere where I ought to have been reserved, spiritless, dull, and deceitful—had I talked only of the weather and the roads, and had I spoken only once in ten minutes, you wouldn't have made fun of me!'

Her mother said, 'My love, don't get offended by Elinor. She was only joking.'

Soon Mrs Dashwood and her daughters were caught up in the local social life. There were the private dances at the park and parties on the boats where Willoughby made his appearance and, in Elinor's eyes, increased his intimacy with the Dashwoods, and Marianne in particular.

When Willoughby was around, Marianne had eyes for no one else. Everything he did was correct and everything he said was smart. When they played cards, he ensured she got a good hand. It was the season of joy for Marianne.

But Elinor was unhappy with it all.

The next day, Marianne delightedly told Elinor that Willoughby had given her a horse as a gift.

'He plans to send his groom to Somersetshire for it,' she added. 'You will share the horse with me!'

***

Colonel Brandon, the Middletons, Willoughby and the Dashwoods planned a visit to Whitwell, an estate that belonged to the Colonel's brother-in-law, but they had to cancel the trip when Brandon announced that he had to go to London on urgent business. The party decided to ride about in the countryside and Marianne later confessed to Elinor that Willoughby took her to his estate at Allenham. Elinor was appalled by her sister's indiscretion. Willoughby visited Barton Cottage and expressed his

great fondness for it. But the next day, Mrs Dashwood and Elinor found Marianne in tears and Willoughby rushing out of the house.

He declared, 'I have to go to London and will probably be away for the rest of the year.'

Marianne did not sleep that night; in fact, she spent most of it crying. Willoughby did not write any of them a letter; Marianne had apparently not even expected one. Mrs Dashwood was surprised and Elinor became uneasy.

A week later, a man approached the cottage on a horse. It was Edward Ferrars. But he kept his distance from the sisters and behaved completely unlike a lover.

Edward talked about his prospects with the Dashwood family.

He said, 'I do not intend to find a job. I would rather be helpless and idle, despite my mother's great expectations. I don't think one needs to be wealthy to be happy.'

Elinor disagreed, 'Wealth is essential for happiness,' she said.

Edward spent a week with them—the time passed swiftly with walks, visits and dances.

Elinor felt that his stay was too short; she hoped she would have him around for a longer period.

Sometime later, Sir John Middleton invited the Steele sisters, Lucy and Anne, who lived in Exeter, and were distantly related to Mrs Jennings. The Dashwood women did not think that they were well behaved but their visitors thought well of their hosts.

One day, Lucy and Elinor were out walking when Lucy asked, 'You will find my query odd, but do you personally know your sister-in-law's mother, Mrs Ferrars?'

Elinor thought it was an odd question.

She answered, 'I have never seen Mrs Ferrars.'

Lucy carried on, 'So you can't tell me what kind of a person she is?'

'No,' replied Elinor cautiously.

'You will find it odd, but I have my reasons for asking this question,' Lucy explained, 'I am engaged to her son.'

Elinor cried out, 'Do you know Mr Robert Ferrars?'

Lucy replied, 'Not Mr Robert Ferrars — his elder brother!'

Elinor was astonished. She looked at Lucy in amazement.

The latter said, 'You may well be surprised. No one in my family knows about it, but we got engaged four years back.'

'Four years!' stunned Elinor exclaimed. She did not know what else to say.

***

Mrs Jennings had a house near Portman Square in London. She was going there in January and asked the elder Dashwood sisters to accompany her. Speaking for her sister, Elinor said no. The alleged reason for not accepting the invitation was their resolution not to leave their mother alone.

Mrs Jennings was surprised and pressed her invitation.

Sir John intervened, and finally the sisters gave their nod. Their mother was delighted.

They left in the first week of January. The Middletons would follow them a week later. The

Steeles remained at the park. After a three-day journey in Mrs Jennings's carriage, they arrived in London. Elinor straight away wrote her mother a letter. Marianne, on the other hand, penned a short note to John Willoughby, telling him about their arrival. She waited for him eagerly and was disappointed when it was Colonel Brandon who turned up that evening, and not Willoughby. Later, Mrs Jennings talked about the bad weather, and Marianne believed that a communication from Willoughby was held up by the rain.

A few days later, there was a knock at the door and Elinor said it was probably Willoughby.

Marianne walked to the door and then returned dejected when she saw that their visitor was Colonel Brandon.

***

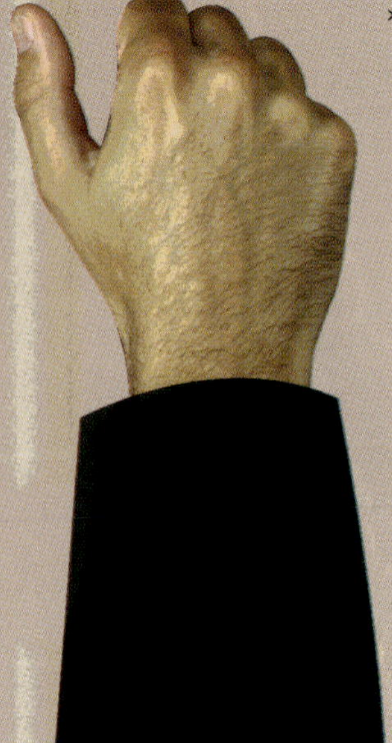

Colonel Brandon visited almost daily. He came to talk with Elinor and look at Marianne.

A week after they came to London, Willoughby's card was seen on the table.

'Goodness!' cried Marianne, 'he came when we were out.'

Elinor said, 'He will come again tomorrow.'

But Willoughby did not come—or even write. Marianne saw him at a party speaking earnestly to somebody else.

She said, 'Why doesn't he look at me?'

Elinor said, 'Probably he hasn't seen you yet.'

At last Willoughby approached them and addressed himself to Elinor—and not Marianne.

He asked about Mrs Dashwood and how long they had been in London. Elinor could not say a word!

'I came last Tuesday, but you were not home.'

'But, did you not receive my notes?' Marianne cried out in anxiety.

He did not immediately reply, but said after a while, 'I received the information you sent,' and turned quickly away.

Marianne, dreadfully white, slumped into her chair. Elinor revived her with lavender water.

Willoughby left behind a letter that said: 'Madam, I want you to understand that my affections were, for a long time, engaged elsewhere.'

Marianne was devastated. She paused over the letter for some time with astonishment and read it over and over again. Mrs Jennings attempted to comfort Marianne but failed.

***

After breakfast the next day, Marianne showed Elinor a letter she received from Willoughby, in which he apologized if his conduct had offended her.

'I have great estimation for the Dashwood family,' he wrote. 'I regret if I gave Marianne reasons to believe that my feelings for her were different than what I thought. I want to tell you that I'm getting engaged soon to a woman whom I love.'

Willoughby enclosed the three notes that Marianne had written to him. When Elinor saw these notes she was surprised for her sister had pleaded with Willoughby to come and see her. But she treated Marianne gently for she understood what she was going through.

Marianne said, 'Let's leave London right now and go home!'

Elinor said, 'We can't leave abruptly. It will hurt Mrs Jennings's feelings.'

Mrs Jennings did her best to cheer up Marianne but she said all the wrong things. For example, she told Elinor, 'Marianne must remember that there are many good young men in the world.'

Mrs Jennings also called some people for dinner to please Marianne, but Marianne's spirits remained low and she left the table early. Thus, she was not there when one of Mrs Jennings's friends said, 'Willoughby wasted his fortune and suddenly proposed to the rich heiress Sophia Grey.'

The following day, Colonel Brandon visited and related to Elinor his own sad love story.

He said, 'I was once in love with a girl named Eliza. But, against her wishes, she was married off to my brother. My brother treated her badly and she deceived him. They got divorced and she went away. Some years later I found her in London. She was sick and dying of consumption. She told me to look after her young daughter. I put the girl in school and Willoughby later seduced her. That's why he rushed off to London on the day we planned our excursion.'

Elinor told Marianne the Colonel's story. But Marianne did not believe her, and was even more

dejected. Mrs Dashwood also wrote a letter to her daughters, in which she stated, 'I am pained and shocked at Willoughby's duplicity. But don't leave London. John is there and will be visiting you shortly.'

Later, Marianne reluctantly yielded to Elinor's entreaties and agreed to go shopping with her and Mrs Jennings.

While they were shopping, Mrs Jennings remembered that she had to meet a lady at the end of the street. So the two sisters entered a crowded shop. They had to wait for an attendant. A gentleman in front of them was taking a long time to decide on a tooth-pick case. When he turned around they saw that it was their brother!

He said that he and Fanny had been in London for the past two days.

'I wanted to visit you yesterday,' he said, 'but we had to take Harry to see the wild beasts at the zoo. We were at Mrs Ferrars's the rest of the day. I will come over tomorrow.'

As they were leaving, Mr Dashwood's sisters introduced him to Mrs Jennings.

He duly visited the next day—with a pretence apology from Fanny who did not come.

'She was very busy with her mother,' John said, and it was left at that.

Later, he went for a walk with Elinor, and made some enquiries.

'Is Colonel Brandon a rich man?'

Elinor answered, 'Yes. He has vast property in Dorsetshire.'

'I am happy for it. He is a gentleman. Elinor, I congratulate you!'

'Brother! What do you mean?'

'He loves you. I have observed him closely. How much is his fortune?'

'I think 2,000 pounds a year. But I know that the Colonel doesn't wish in the least to marry me!'

'You are wrong, Elinor.'

Elinor changed the topic and made her own enquiries.

'Is Mr Edward Ferrars getting married?'

'Not really; it's not settled.'

***

The next time John visited his sisters at Mrs Jennings, he said to Elinor, 'I will be pleased if you were to marry Colonel Brandon.'

Elinor answered, 'I assure you dear brother that I don't have any intention of marrying the man.'

But John was insistent.

'It will be a good match,' he said.

He then changed the topic to the Ferrars.

'Mrs Ferrars wants her son Edward to marry the rich Miss Morton,' he said.

Fanny Dashwood wasn't too keen on visiting Mrs Jennings but after John spoke well of her, she agreed to go. In fact, Fanny enjoyed Mrs Jennings' company.

'I'll host a party for you at my house in Harley Street. I hope you will also come,' she told Elinor and Marianne.

Her guest list included Colonel Brandon, the Middletons and Mrs Ferrars. Elinor feared that she may have to meet Edward at the party and was relieved when she learned that he would not be coming. At the party, Elinor took an immediate dislike to Mrs Ferrars, who only cared about getting her son married to a rich woman.

***

After much persuasion, Marianne agreed to travel to the house of Mrs Palmer, a friend of Mrs Jennings, in Cleveland. She began to take an interest in day-to-day activities, when she suddenly fell ill.

Mrs Palmers's doctor who attended to Marianne said she had an infection. This scared Mrs Palmer, who had recently given birth to a baby boy. So she took the baby and left for her mother's house. Her husband soon followed, and the group grew smaller.

As Marianne's condition grew worse over the next few days, Elinor decided to seek Colonel Brandon's assistance.

The Colonel agreed to go and fetch Mrs Dashwood. The doctor was summoned, but medicines did not help much.

Elinor kept watch over her sister—and was rewarded when Marianne began to show signs of recovery.

Eventually, the doctor officially told them that Marianne was now out of danger.

Elinor now kept a look-out for her mother and Colonel Brandon. One night, she heard a bustle in the hall, Elinor jumped up. She ran to the door—and there stood Willoughby!

***

Elinor stared at him in horror. It was highly inappropriate for him to be visiting them at all, leave alone in the middle of the night.

'Miss Dashwood, I beg you to hear me,' he said.

'No,' she replied emphatically.

'I have to speak to you only!'

'Well, be quick!'

'Is your sister out of danger?' he asked.

'I hope so.'

'I want apologize for my earlier behaviour,' he said, and added, 'and yes, I am drunk.'

'Marianne forgave you long ago,' Elinor said.

When he began to relate his side of the story, which

wasn't very sincere, Elinor contemptuously said, 'It's useless, telling me your side of the story.'

He went on, 'I never had a large fortune. I have always associated with very rich people. This increased my debts. I married Miss Sophia Grey for her money. I don't love her. I have the highest regard for Marianne.'

***

By the time Colonel Brandon arrived at Cleveland with Mrs Dashwood, Marianne's condition had improved. They were very happy.

Mrs Dashwood told Elinor that, on the drive to Cleveland, the Colonel had made a surprising confession.

'He said he is in love with Marianne and wants to marry her. I will do all that I can to help this match fructify.'

Marianne got better and better with every passing day. Mrs Dashwood's spirits rose.

'My Elinor, you cannot understand my happiness,' she said.

***

As Marianne's health had improved vastly, the Dashwoods decided to return to Barton Cottage.

Soon, Marianne felt strong enough to take a walk with Elinor. The topic of Willoughby came up and Marianne said, 'I behaved unwisely. I should have conducted myself in a better way.'

Elinor consoled her sister and told her about Willoughby's confession. Marianne was relieved to hear that Willoughby did what he did for financial reasons and wasn't truly a deceitful person.

Marianne said, 'Anyway, I don't think I would have been happy with him. He lacks integrity.'

Later, Elinor told Mrs Dashwood about Willoughby's confession as well.

Mrs Dashwood said, 'I pity the man, but I cannot forgive him for the way he treated my daughter.' Just then, the family's manservant, Thomas, arrived bearing interesting news.

'Mr Ferrars has married Lucy Steele,' he said.

Both Marianne and Elinor were distressed by the news.

'Thomas, did she tell you in so many words that she was married?'

'Yes, Madam. She said she had changed her name before she came here.'

'Was Mr Ferrars with her?'

'Yes. He was in the carriage, with his back to me.'

Mrs Dashwood shared her daughters' distress. She wondered if she had not paid enough attention to Elinor; whether she did not feel for her eldest daughter or thought about Elinor's feelings during the past few months.

The time went by, until, one day, Elinor saw someone approaching their house on horseback. She thought it was Colonel Brandon, but it was actually Edward Ferrars! Edward entered the house and the Dashwood sisters immediately began to question him.

Elinor said, 'I want to enquire about Mrs Edward Ferrars!'

But she did not get up. Mrs Dashwood and Marianne both looked earnestly at him.

He looked perplexed for a while, and then finally said, 'Oh! You mean Lucy?' and proceeded to tell them the whole story.

He had rashly asked Lucy Steele to marry him all those years ago, but had later fallen in love with Elinor. However, he had to honour his engagement to Lucy Steele, since he had given her his word. Once, at some party, Lucy's sister Anne mentioned to his mother how excited she was about soon becoming part of the family.

'As soon as mother heard of my engagement, she threatened to disown me if I did not marry Miss Morton. I refused, and she disinherited me in favour of my brother,' he said.

Then, Lucy—whose main attraction was money—shifted her attentions to Edward's brother Robert, who would now inherit the family fortune.

This bit of information greatly relieved Elinor. She rushed out of the room and shed tears of joy! Edward stayed and spoke about several personal things before he got down to the subject that was close to his heart: he proposed to Elinor, and the latter, with great happiness, accepted his proposal.

Edward stayed for dinner and told them about the unfortunate circumstances that resulted in him getting engaged to Lucy Steele.

'Indeed, Lucy sent me a note telling me about her engagement to my brother Robert,' he confessed. 'In the same note, she said she was breaking all relations with me.'

Things moved at a fast pace. Colonel Barton came to Barton Cottage and was thrilled at the news of Edward's and Elinor's engagement. He invited them to Delaford parsonage—which he had offered to Edward when he was engaged to Lucy Steele—so that the couple could live in comfort. Mrs Ferrars, on her part, reconciled herself to the fact that Edward was happy to marry Elinor. So Edward and Elinor got married and took up their new residence at Delaford, and frequently invited Colonel Brandon and Marianne to visit them.

Edward and Elinor hoped that the Colonel and Marianne would get attached to one another. Which they did! Eventually, Colonel Brandon and Marianne got married and went to live at Delaford. Elinor and Marianne, and their husbands, maintained their close relations with Mrs Dashwood and Margaret, who were happily settled at Barton Cottage. All the families lived happily ever after.

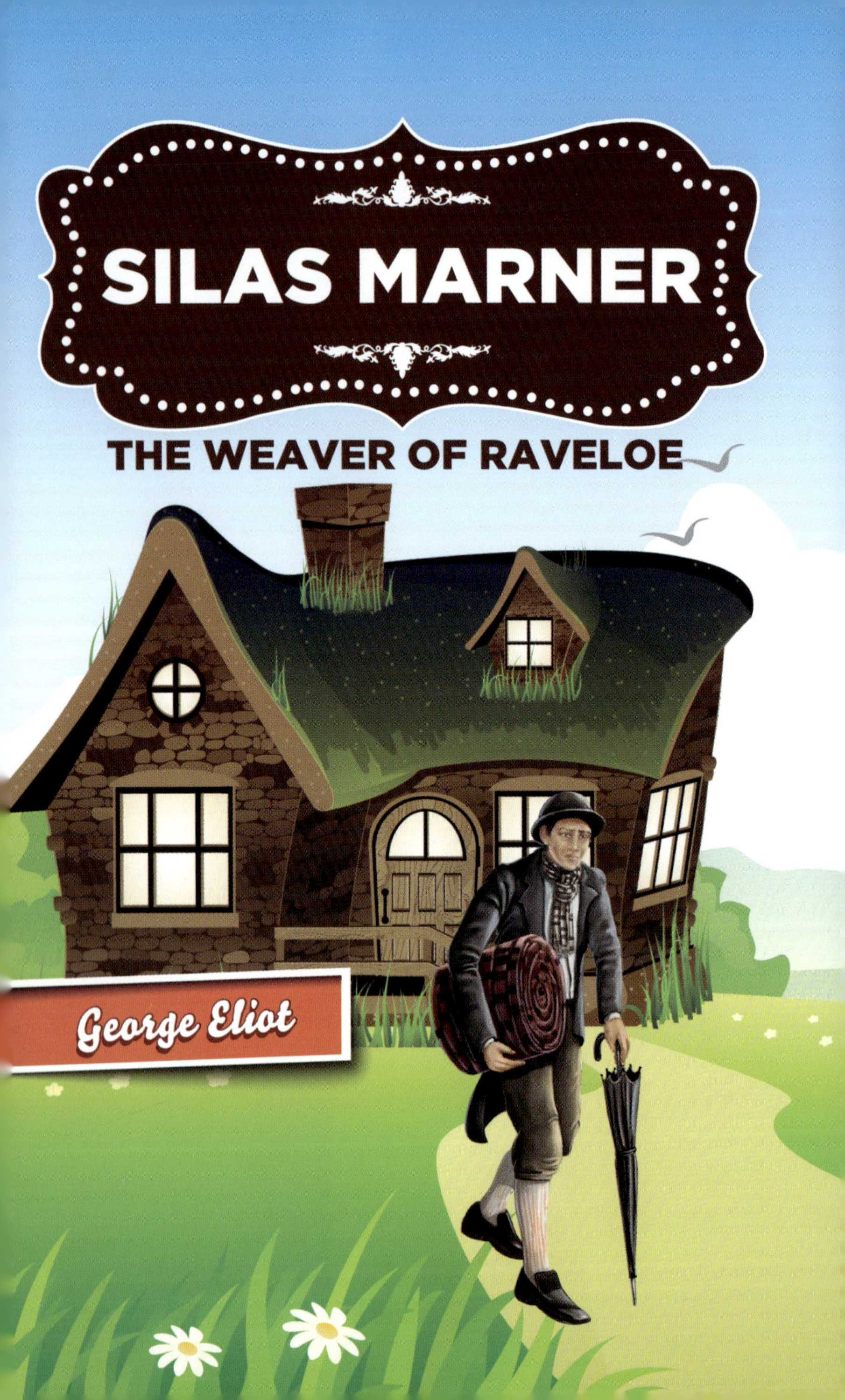

# SILAS MARNER

## THE WEAVER OF RAVELOE

George Eliot

Silas Marner was a linen-weaver who worked in a stone cottage called near the hedgerows close to the village of Raveloe. The dubious noise from Silas's loom was in stark contrast to the cheerful sound of a winnowing machine, or the rhythmic clatter of the flail and the boys of Raveloe thus had a fascination for it.

They would often leave their birds'-nesting or nutting to look at Silas's loom and the man himself at work. Sometimes Silas would come out and stare at them so sternly that they would scurry away! Fifteen years had passed since Silas had left Lantern Yard and arrived in Raveloe.

Back in Lantern Yard, Silas Marner had been friends with a young man named William Dane. Others may have seen faults in Dane, but not Silas. Silas's fiancée Sarah tolerated the few times when William occasionally sat with them at Sunday services.

Silas was prone to cataleptic fits—where his entire body would go completely stiff. When one of these fits occurred at a prayer meeting, William observed that it seemed like a visitation of the Devil. His comment pained Silas.

Worse, Sarah began to act indifferently towards him, but denied that she wanted to call off their engagement.

Once, when the senior deacon fell critically ill, the members of the community took turns to stay with him at night. Silas and William also did so, taking shifts in which one would relieve the other at two o'clock in the morning.

The night that the deacon died, William was supposed to relieve Silas at two. Instead, he only showed up at six, with the minister, who accused Silas of theft.

Silas's pocket knife was produced as evidence—it had been found near the box from which the bag containing all the church money that had been stolen.

Silas was speechless at the accusation, but eventually managed to stutter that he was innocent. However, when the townspeople searched the whole area, William found the empty bag behind Silas's cupboard!

William asked Silas to confess and the latter looked at him reproachfully, 'You have known me for nine years; I have not lied once during that time. But God will surely clear my name.'

Silas added, 'I remember, I was not even carrying the knife!'

He looked at William pointedly and said, 'I last used the knife to cut you a strap, and I did not put it back in my pocket. You, William, robbed the money and hatched a plot to blame me!'

But the community had already decided he was guilty. Sarah broke her engagement with Silas and, a month later, married William. This was when Silas Marner left town.

***

Silas worked long and hard, now in the heart of Raveloe town, to complete Mrs Osgood's order for linen. He wove like a spider, impulsively and without thinking, and Mrs Osgood paid him in gold. For the first time in his life, Silas saw five shining guineas in his hand!

One day, when he was still new in Raveloe, Silas noticed that Sally Oates, the cobbler's wife, was suffering from the same illness that led to his own mother's death. He recalled that his mother had found relief when given a medicine made from foxglove, and thus cured her. Soon after, Silas was surrounded by mothers seeking a cure for whooping cough, and rheumatics and other ailments. They paid him in silver and Silas could have run a profitable business in drugs as well as charms! But he was not tempted by money; he could never be false to himself.

However, when he chased away would-be patients in irritation, the people—who had thought he had a magic cure for all ills—stopped coming to meet him. In fact, his isolation only increased.

The years passed, and Silas Marner lived in solitude. His savings increased, but his life narrowed and hardened. His life was now just a function of weaving and collecting money without a thought of the end results.

***

Squire Cass, Raveloe's lone Squire, lived in a big mansion called Red House near the church.

His wife had died many years ago but he had several sons whom he kept at home idle. However, one son, named Dunstan—also known as Dunsey Cass—was a jeering, spiteful chap who liked his drinks, who only barely managed to keep his family name intact.

The eldest son, Godfrey, was a fine, good-natured young man. He was currently courting a gentle lady named Miss Nancy Lattimer. Unfortunately, he had recently started behaving like his younger brother. One evening, Godfrey called for Dunsey. The younger brother entered the room, drunk, and asked what he wanted.

'I want the 100 pounds rent that you took from the Fowlers. I need to give it to the Squire. You know what he'll do if he finds out that you used up the rent money.'

Dunsey sneered, 'I can tell the Squire and Miss Nancy that his handsome, eldest son secretly married Molly Farren, and is so unhappy that his new wife is addicted to alcohol and opium, that he cannot live with her.'

The twenty-six-year-old Godfrey had, in fact, impulsively married Molly in secret. Dunstan saw in this degrading marriage, the means to trap his brother.

Godfrey retorted, 'Molly has been threatening to tell the Squire anyway, so your secrecy has no value at all! In fact, I'll tell the Squire myself—and you can go to the devil!'

***

Dunsey decided to sell his horse, Wildfire, the next morning. But that night, he went for a ride and being rather drunk, met with an accident. The horse fell on a stake and died.

As Dunsey passed Silas Marner's house on his way home, his thoughts drifted to the money that Silas supposedly had stashed in his house. He decided to visit Silas when he saw a light in the house, and entered when he saw that the door was open. No one appeared to be at home and Dunsey started doing some exploring.

A fire was blazing inside and dinner was cooking. Dunsey wondered where Silas was. As he looked around, Dunsey saw a patch

in the floor that was covered with sand. When he swept away the sand and lifted the loose bricks, he found leather bags. Dunsey was sure these bags were filled with gold! So he took them and fled.

***

Silas returned home and thought nothing about the unlocked door—nobody had stolen anything from him before. So, when he sat down to have his meal, he noticed nothing amiss.

However, he had a habit of counting his money every night. So after dinner, he removed the bricks—and found an empty hole when he put his hand in to pull out the bags! He frantically searched everywhere in the cottage and finally realized that someone had stolen his money. He let out a wild scream of anguish and tried to think who could have taken his gold. He thought about likely robbers and the name of Jem Rodney, a local poacher, came to his mind.

Silas decided to confide in the town's important people, but they had all gone to a party at Mrs Osgood's house. The Rainbow tavern and the village inn were all almost empty.

Anyway, Silas told the few people in the tavern what had happened. At first, no one believed him. The landlord asked Jem Rodney, who was sitting there, to hold Silas down. But Silas turned on Rodney and asked him to return the money he had stolen. Rodney reacted angrily and told Silas not to accuse him.

After a while, everyone calmed down, and Mr Dowlas asked Silas how much money was robbed.

Silas answered, 'More than 270 pounds.'

The suspicion his listeners had when they first listened to Silas's story, melted away because of the simple and straightforward manner in which he related the events to them.

It was not possible for his neighbours to disbelieve Marner's tale. There was no reason he would tell lies, and, as Mr Macey observed, 'Folks that were backed by the devil, were unlikely to be in such bad shape,' as the unfortunate Silas.

The landlord said, 'It could not have been Jem Rodney who committed this act, Master Marner.

Jem may be guilty of poaching a rabbit or a hare, but he would not commit a job like this. Besides, Jem has been sitting in this tavern all evening, as he usually does.'

'Yes, yes,' Mr Macey said. 'We must not accuse innocent folk. The law doesn't work that way. There has to be hard evidence and people who will swear against a man before the law can act against him.'

Silas went up to Jem and said, 'Jem, there's no evidence against you. Since you've been to my house several times, I suspected you. I shouldn't have done that.'

***

When Godfrey came back from Mrs Osgood's party that night, he wasn't surprised to see that his brother had not yet come home. Maybe he had not found a buyer for Wildfire, and was looking for one; or maybe, it being a foggy afternoon, he was staying in the nearby town. Godfrey was also distracted by his own problems with his old love, Nancy Lammeter, and Molly. Besides, Dunsey did not care about keeping Godfrey updated anyway, so Godfrey did not give it too much thought.

Everyone in town discussed Silas Marner's misfortune the next morning. Godfrey and others visited his home to collect evidence and gossip. A tinderbox was found and somehow linked to the crime. Some villagers thought that Silas had gone mad and was lying about the robbery.

The landlord of the tavern Mr Snell, said, 'A peddler had visited Raveloe sometime back; he carried a tinderbox.'

But, Silas said, 'The peddler never entered my cottage.'

Godfrey's attention strayed because of Dunsey's absence. He decided to find out the fate of his horse Wildfire, and met Bryce—the man who wanted to buy the animal. Bryce was surprised by Dunsey's disappearance and told Godfrey that the horse had been found dead.

Godfrey then decided to tell his father everything, but later developed cold feet and kept the news of his marriage a secret.

So Godfrey confessed about Wildfire and how he had given Dunsey money from the rent. Squire Cass was enraged. He blamed his financial problems on his sons' overindulgence.

The weeks went by; there was no sign of Dunsey and nobody suspected him of the robbery, the peddler continued to be the prime suspect.

Poor Silas kept on weaving but he felt no joy in his work. The villagers took pity on him and brought him food.

✳✳✳

Nancy Lammeter arrived at the Squire's Red House, along with her father, for the New Year's dance. She was irritated when Godfrey helped her get out of the carriage. Nancy had made it obvious that she would not marry Godfrey and she found his attention annoying.

But when the Squire asked Godfrey to dance the first dance with Nancy, Godfrey was embarrassed but he asked her and she accepted.

Godfrey was aware that Nancy cared for him. But he told Nancy that she was cold-hearted in the hope of provoking a quarrel. Nancy's sister Priscilla, however, arrived at that moment to repair Nancy's dress.

Godfrey did not know it, but at that very moment Molly was on her way on foot to Raveloe, their baby in her arms. Godfrey had told Molly he would rather die than accept her as his wife. She planned to gatecrash the party to avenge herself against Godfrey. Molly felt that, if Godfrey gave her some of his money, she would be able to get over her addiction of opium and alcohol.

Molly had been on her feet from the morning and, by evening, she was too weak to even stand.

She took some opium to get relief but the drug only made her drowsy and she soon feel unconscious, still clutching her child.

The child saw a light close by—it was Silas's cottage—and went towards it. She found the door open, and wandered in. Silas did not notice her at first, since he was in the middle of one of his fits when she came in. By the time he saw her, she was fast asleep in front of the fire. He traced her tracks backwards and soon found Molly lying in the snow.

As the men and women were dancing at the Red House, Silas Marner entered with Godfrey's child in his arms. The Squire got angry and asked Silas why he had intruded on a private party. Silas said he needed a doctor for a woman who was lying in the snow.

Sensing that the woman was Molly, Godfrey got alarmed and thought she could be alive!

Adamantly, Godfrey accompanied Kimble, the doctor. On the way they picked up Dolly Winthrop, wife of the wheelwright, to act as a nurse. Godfrey was deeply worried. If Molly was alive, he would have to confess the truth.

Kimble said, 'She has been dead for several hours.'

Godfrey went in to see her and confirm that she indeed was Molly.

Silas said, 'I want to keep the child. She will make up for the gold I lost! I don't know where my money went and I don't know where this child came from!'

Godfrey gave Silas some money for he was determined that his child should be well looked after.

Molly got a pauper's burial and the villagers were amazed that Silas was keen to keep the child. This increased their sympathy for him. Dolly helped Silas a great deal. She gave him clothes and took care of the child.

Dolly persuaded Silas to get the girl baptized and he thought that Eppie was a good, short name for her. Silas and Eppie got baptized together. Eppie was curious and made demands on Silas. His gold had kept him indoors but Eppie tempted Silas to enjoy the outdoors.

Thanks to the girl, Silas bonded with the villagers like never before. Though Godfrey kept his distance from the Marner house, he kept a close eye on all the action there, especially that of his daughter.

***

Sixteen years passed. Godfrey had married Nancy, Squire Cass had died and his inheritance was split up among his relatives. Silas Marner was among the congregation that filed out of the church that Sunday morning. He looked older than his fifty-five years. Eppie had turned eighteen and looked quite pretty. She walked alongside Silas, and Aaron Winthrop—Dolly's son—followed eagerly.

Silas's cottage now had a cat, a dog and a kitten. There was another room too, courtesy Godfrey.

The townspeople regarded Silas as an 'exceptional man'.

Silas had discussed with Eppie the fact that he was not her father; how he had found her and brought her up. Eppie told him she considered him the best father in Raveloe though she would like to know more about her mother. Silas gave her Molly's wedding ring.

The Red House had gained a domestic feel, but lacked a child and this rankled Godfrey.

Nancy invited her father and Priscilla to take tea at the Red House. Priscilla had assumed the running of the Lammeter farm from her father who was now getting old. Before Priscilla left Nancy's house, she went for a walk with Nancy in the garden. There Nancy mentioned that Godfrey was not happy with their family life. This fact angered Priscilla. Nancy, however, rushed to the defence of her husband. She said that it quite a natural thing; he was disappointed because they did not have any children.

When Godfrey went on his regular Sunday walk around the Red House grounds, he left Nancy with her thoughts. Nancy pondered on their not having any children and the distress that this fact had brought to Godfrey. They had had a daughter, but this child died at birth. Nancy wondered if she was doing the right thing by resisting Godfrey's idea that they adopt a child.

Nancy had been quite adamant in this matter. She had insisted that it wasn't the right thing to obtain something which Providence had not given. She predicted that adopted children invariably don't turn out to be good people.

Nancy's stubborn opposition to adopting a child was not based on any specific reason, but only because she felt that it was important to have 'her own little code'. Godfrey had argued that Eppie, who Silas Marner had adopted, had turned out to be a good child. But his argument bore no weight. Godfrey never thought that Silas would object, and so had decided to adopt Eppie if Nancy every agreed to the idea.

Godfrey always believed that Nancy could not bear him children because he had not claimed Eppie as his daughter. Adopting her would make amends for his earlier fault. Godfrey saw that, in adopting her, he would find a way to make up for his earlier irresponsibility.

***

The Red House door opened and Godfrey returned from his walk. There was happiness in Nancy's eyes when she looked around from the window where she was standing.

'I'm so happy you have come,' she said as she approached him. 'I started to get…'

She stopped speaking because Godfrey's hands were trembling when he kept his hat down. He looked at his wife with a face that had turned white and gave her a mystifying glance, as if he only saw her as a segment of a scene that she could not see.

Nancy put her hand on his and dared to talk. He did not feel her touch and flung himself into his chair.

Jane, the maid, entered the room with an urn that hissed with hot water.

'Tell Jane to stay away,' said Godfrey.

When the maid closed the door behind her, he began to speak to Nancy.

'Sit down there,' he said, pointing to a chair near him. 'I returned soon so you would hear it from me first. I've experienced a terrible shock. But I'm afraid it will be a greater shock to you.'

'Is it about my father or Priscilla?' Nancy asked, her lips quivering. She clasped her hands tightly on her lap.

'No, it's about Dunstan,' said Godfrey, not being able to reveal his thoughts in the skilled manner he wished he had. 'It's my brother Dunstan, who disappeared sixteen years ago. We have found him! Rather, we have found his skeleton!'

The words came as a sort of relief to Nancy. She sat calmly and heard what Godfrey had to say.

'The stone pit has been dried and after the draining… he's lain there all this time—possibly for sixteen years, stuck between two huge stones. We found his seals and … and my gold-plated hunting whip which has my name on it. He had taken it without telling me on that day when he went on a hunt on Wildfire. It was the last time that anyone saw him.'

Godfrey paused. It was tough to relate what happened next.

'Did he drown himself, what do you think?' asked Nancy.

She was now wondering why Godfrey was so deeply shaken about something that had taken place so many years ago, and that too to an unloved brother.

'No, he fell into the pit,' explained Godfrey, in a soft but clear voice, as if the words conveyed a very deep meaning. Then he added, 'Dunstan was the person who robbed Silas Marner!'

The blood rushed up in Nancy's neck and face at this astonishing revelation. She had been brought up to think that even a distant relationship with crime was a great dishonour.

'Godfrey!' she exclaimed.

There was compassion in her voice for she realized the dishonour that her husband must be feeling so sharply right now!

'The weaver's money was found in the pit, all of it—intact!' Godfrey continued. 'They've collected it all and they are taking the remains of Dunsey to the Rainbow. I returned to tell you the facts.'

He stared at the ground for some minutes, not saying a word. Nancy refrained from saying any comforting words. She had an instinctive feeling that there was something else that Godfrey wanted to tell her. Godfrey raised his eyes to look at her face. He looked directly at her and said, 'Nancy, everything is eventually found out, at some time or the other. When God wishes it, our secrets get spilled out. I have lived for many years with one thing on my mind. I won't keep that secret from you anymore.'

Nancy's worst fears returned. The couple's eyes met uneasily.

'Nancy, when I married you, I hid a fact from you. I should have told you before: the woman who Marner found in the snow dead—Eppie's mother—was my lawfully wedded wife. Eppie is my daughter!'

Godfrey halted. He dreaded the effect this confession would have on Nancy. But she sat still, though her eyes fell and did not meet his. She became pale and silent as a statue and clasped her hands together.

After some time Godfrey said in a trembling voice, 'You won't think of me the same again.'

Nancy remained silent.

'I should not have left the child alone. But I could never have given you up, Nancy. I suffered a lot for it.'

Nancy raised her eyes and said, without indignation, but with regret.

'If you had told me this six years ago, we could have adopted the child.'

'Nancy, I'm a worse person than what you felt I was,' said Godfrey. 'Please forgive me!'

'You've made amends by being good to me for fifteen years, Godfrey. Now it's up to me.'

'We can adopt Eppie now,' said Godfrey. 'I don't mind what the world says about it. I'll be open and honest forever.'

'She's a big girl now,' said Nancy and shook her head in sadness.

'But you have to acknowledge her and look after her. I'll do my best for her, and ask God to love me.'

'Let's go to Silas Marner's house tonight itself.'

***

After the excitement of finding his gold, Silas sat with Eppie in their home that evening. Silas had sent Aaron and Dolly away. He wanted solitude with Eppie.

Silas thought about the discovery of his money and replayed the events that had taken place since its disappearance. He told Eppie that he loved her very much and the money would go to her.

Eppie said, 'If it had not been for you, I would have landed in the workhouse.'

There was a knock on the door and when Eppie opened it, she found Godfrey and Nancy

Cass there. Godfrey told Silas that he wished to make amends for what Dunsey did and also repay Silas for another debt.

Godfrey said to Silas, 'The money that you have regained is insufficient for you to live comfortably. You will need to keep on working.'

Silas said, 'The money I have may seem little to a rich gentleman, but it's more than what most people have.'

Godfrey replied, 'Eppie wasn't born to live a working life. It would be nice if she lived in a place like my home.'

When he heard these words, Silas became anxious.

Godfrey said, 'Nancy and I don't have any children. Therefore we would like Eppie to come and stay with us as our daughter.'

Godfrey thought that Silas would be happy to see Eppie live in such conditions. He promised Silas that he too would be provided for.

Eppie saw that Silas was upset at hearing these words.

Silas told her to choose the life she wanted to live and she told Godfrey and his wife, 'I don't want to leave my father. I don't want to be a lady.'

Godfrey then confessed that he was her father, and so had some claim on her.

Silas got angry and retorted, 'If that's the case, Godfrey, you should have taken Eppie when she was a child and not waited until Eppie and I had grown to love one another.'

Godfrey did not expect this resistance.

'Silas, you are standing in the way of Eppie's happiness,' he said. Silas left the decision to Eppie.

Nancy sympathized with Eppie and Silas, but felt that that Eppie must claim what was rightfully hers. Eppie, however, said that she preferred to live with Silas.

Nancy said, 'It's your duty to live in your real father's home.'

But Eppie was adamant.

'Silas is my real father,' she said.

Discouraged, Godfrey and Nancy left and said that they would return some other day.

***

When they returned home, Godfrey accepted that Silas was right. He resigned himself to just helping his daughter from a distance. Godfrey and his wife assumed that Eppie would marry Aaron.

Godfrey felt that the dislike that Eppie showed towards him was a result of his disregarding her for so many years.

The next morning Silas told Eppie, 'I want to go to Lantern Yard, my old home, to clear some questions pertaining to the theft for which I had to pay a heavy price.'

When he reached the old town, much had changed. He looked for the old chapel but found that it no longer existed. In its place was a big factory.

Silas realized that Raveloe was where he now belonged and he headed back there. Upon returning, he told Dolly that he would be unable to prove his innocence, and Dolly said, 'It does not matter if your questions stay unanswered, for nothing changes the fact that you were always right.'

Silas said, 'I have Eppie now. This gives me great faith.'

***

The sun finally shone brightly in Silas Marner's life. On a lovely summer's day,

his daughter married Aaron. Priscilla Lammeter
and her father were among those who attended
the ceremony. Aaron and his bride walked in a
procession in the village. Godfrey had gone out
of town for some 'special reason' and Priscilla was
there to give her sister company.

Priscilla told her father, 'I wish
Nancy had found a daughter like Eppie
to bring up as her own flesh and blood.'

The marriage procession made a
halt at Mr Macey's house. The church

clerk was too old to attend the wedding festivities but had prepared a speech for Silas Marner.

'Master Marner,' Mr Macey said in a quavering voice, 'I've lived to see my prediction come true. I had said, first among all, that you had no malice in you. I also said that you would get your stolen gold back.'

As the bridal party approached, a loud cheer was heard in the yard of the Rainbow.

As for Eppie, she was thrilled that now she had a large garden—the alterations had been done by Mr Cass.

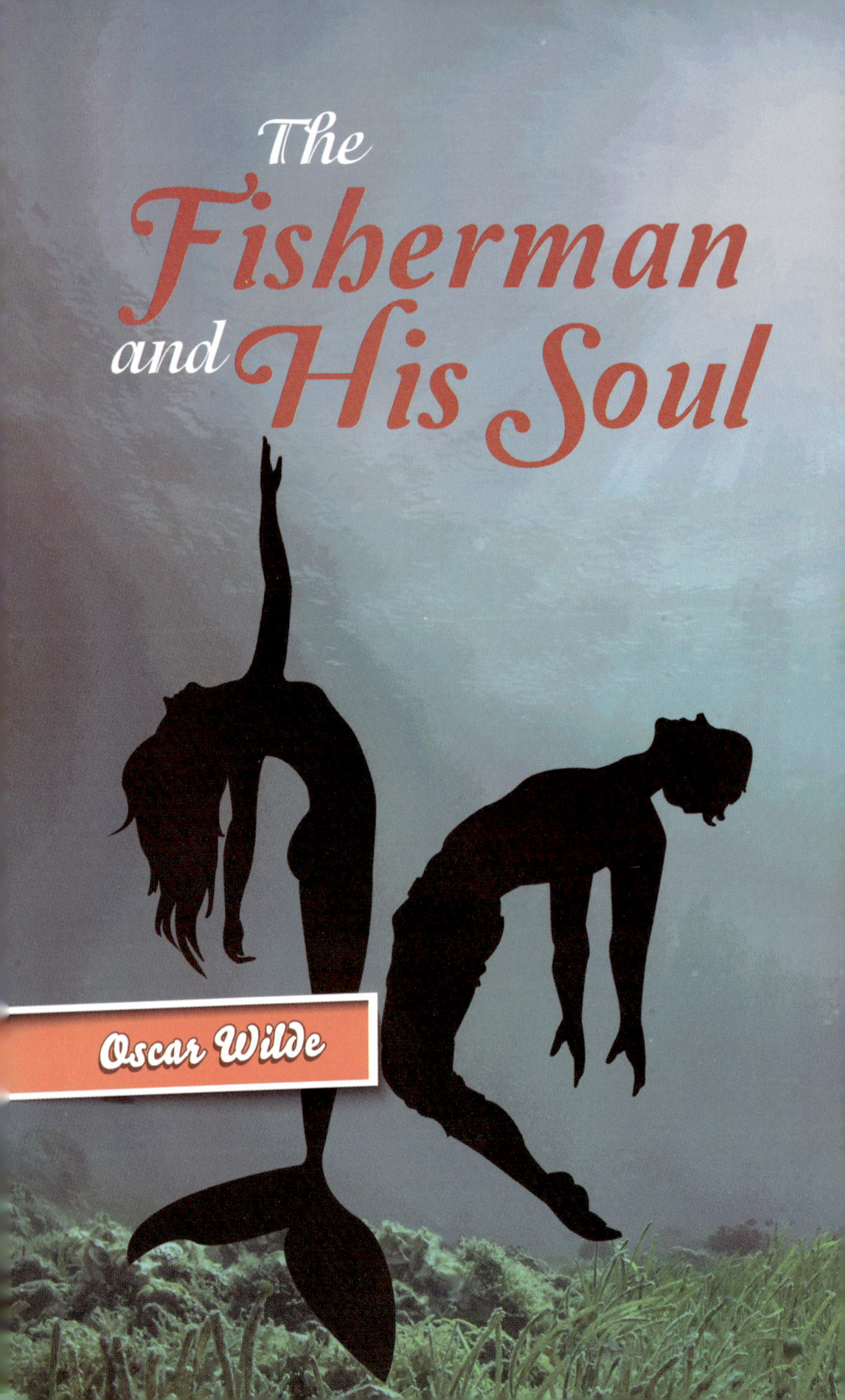
The
Fisherman
and His Soul
Oscar Wilde

Every evening the Fisherman went out upon the sea, and threw his nets into the water.

When the wind blew from the land he caught nothing, or just a little, since it was a bitter wind that rough waves rose up to meet. However, when the wind blew to the shore, the fish came in from the deep, and swam into his nets, and he took them to the market and sold them.

One evening the net was so heavy that hardly could he draw it into the boat. He laughed and said to himself, 'Surely, I have caught all the fish in the sea, or some monster.'

Then, he pulled on the thin ropes, and the net slowly rose to the surface.

It did not contain any fish, or even a monster. Instead, inside the nets, lay a little mermaid, fast asleep.

Her hair was a wet fleece of gold; her body, white as ivory; her tail was of silver and pearl; and her lips were like coral.

She was so beautiful that, when the Fisherman saw her, he was filled with wonder, and drew the net close to him. Then, he leaned over the side and clasped her in his arms. At his touch, she gave a cry like a startled seagull and woke, and looked at him in terror. She struggled to escape, but he could not let her go.

When she found that she could not escape, she wept and said, 'Please let me go. I am the only daughter of a king, and my father is old and alone.'

But the Fisherman answered, 'I will let you go, but only if you promise to come whenever I call you. The fish love to listen to the song of the sea-folk, and so my nets will be full.'

'Will you really let me go if I promise this?' asked the mermaid.

'Absolutely,' he said.

So she promised, and he allowed her to sink into the water, trembling with a strange fear.

Every evening, when the Fisherman went out to sea, and called to the mermaid, she rose out of the water and sang to him. Round and round her swam the dolphins, and the wild gulls circled above her head.

***

As she sang her fabulous songs, all the fish came in from the deep to listen to her, and the Fisherman caught them. And when his boat was laden, the mermaid would sink down into the sea, smiling at him.

However, she did not allow him to touch her. Often, he called to her and pleaded with her to come to him, but she would not. If he tried to catch her, she would dive into the water, and not appear again all that day.

Each day, her voice became sweeter to him. Soon, he was so charmed by the sound of her voice that he did not even think of the fish swimming around him, let alone catch them.

Eventually, one evening, he called to her, and said, 'Little Mermaid, I love you!' and asked her to marry him.

But the Mermaid shook her head. 'You have a human soul. Send your soul away, and I shall love you.'

The Fisherman thought for a while. He said to himself, 'Of what use is my soul to me? I cannot see it. I cannot touch it. I do not know it. I will definitely send it away and then be happy.' He had thus made his decision.

He stood up in the rocking boat, turned to the mermaid and said, 'I will send my soul away, and marry you. And we can live together in the depth of the oceans, where I shall witness everything you sing about, and do everything that you desire of me. We will never be apart again!'

The little Mermaid laughed.

'But how shall I send my soul from me?' cried the Fisherman.

'Alas! I do not know that; the sea folk have no souls,' said the little mermaid, and sank into the water, looking regretfully at him.

***

Early next morning, the Fisherman went to the priest's house and said, 'Father, I am in love with a mermaid and my soul obstructs me from marrying her. Please tell me how I can send away my soul. I do not need it. Of what value is my soul to me? I cannot see it. I cannot touch it and I do not know it.'

The priest beat his breast, and answered, 'Alas! Are you mad? Or are you ill? The soul is the noblest part of man, which was given to us by God. There is nothing more precious than a human soul. It is more precious than all the gold and jewels in the world. Therefore, my son, don't think of this any further, for it is an unforgivable sin.'

The Fisherman's eyes filled with tears when he heard the priest's bitter words.

He said, 'Father, what does my soul profit me, if it stands between me and that which I love?'

At this, the priest gave up and drove the Fisherman from his house without blessing him.

Next, the Fisherman went to the market; he walked slowly, his head bowed in sorrow. The merchants saw him coming, and came to him, one by one.

'What do you have to sell?' they asked.

And when he said he wanted to sell his soul, they laughed at him and told him it was 'not even worth a clipped piece of silver'.

This confused the Fisherman. 'How could this be?' he asked himself. 'The priest tells me that the soul is worth all the gold in the world, and the merchants tell me it is totally worthless.'

Then he left the market and went to the seashore, and thought about his options.

By noon, he remembered that one of his friends had once told him about a young witch who was very cunning. He was so eager to get rid of his soul that he immediately started running to the cave in which she lived. He ran so fast, a cloud of dust followed him.

By the itching of her palm the young witch knew he was coming. She laughed, let down her red hair and stood waiting at the opening of her cave.

'What do you want? What do you want?' she cried, as he came panting up the steep, and bent down before her. 'Fish for your net? A great storm to bring up sunken treasure? Do you want the queen to fall in love with you, I can give you anything! There is a price boy, there is a price, but tell me your wish and I shall give it to you.'

'My desire is just a little thing,' said the Fisherman, 'but no one is willing to help me. So, I have come to you, even though people say you are evil. Whatever your price, I will pay it.'

When he told her what he wanted, the witch grew pale and shivered. She hid her face in her blue mantle, and whispered, 'Pretty boy, pretty boy… that's a terrible thing to do.'

He tossed his brown curls and laughed.

'My soul is nothing to me,' he answered. 'I cannot see it. I may not touch it. I do not know it.'

'What will you give me if I tell you?' asked the witch.

The Fisherman promised to give her everything he owned.

She laughed mockingly at him, and said, 'I can turn the autumn leaves into gold,' she answered, 'I do not need your things.'

'Then what will you take?' he cried.

The witch touched his hair. 'You must dance with me,' she murmured, and smiled at him as she spoke.

'Is that all?' the Fisherman asked.

'That is all,' the witch said, but added that he would have to dance with her 'when the moon is full'.

Then she saw all round, and listened. There was no sound other than that of a wave bothering the smooth pebbles below. So she reached out her hand, and drew him near to her and whispered in his ear, 'Come to the top of the mountain tonight. It is a Sabbath and He will be there.'

The Fisherman was startled.

'Who is this "He" you speak of?' he asked.

She laughed and said, 'That does not matter. Just go tonight, and wait for me under the hornbeam tree. If a black dog runs towards you, hit it with a willow rod, and it will go away. If an owl speaks to you, ignore it. I will come when the moon is full, and we shall dance together on the grass.'

'If I do that, do you promise to tell me how to send away my soul?' he asked again.

She moved out into the sunlight, and the wind rippled through her red hair.

'By the hoofs of the goat I swear it,' she answered.

'Then I shall certainly dance with you. Oh! You are the best witch!' the Fisherman cried happily.

Then he removed his hat to her and left.

***

That evening, the Fisherman climbed to the top of the mountain, and stood under the hornbeam. A great owl, with yellow sulphurous eyes, called to him by his name, but he ignored it. A black dog ran towards him and growled. He hit it with a rod of willow, and it went away crying.

At midnight, the witches came flying through the air like bats.

'Phew!' they cried, as they got off, 'there is someone here we do not know!'

They chattered to each other, and made signs. Finally, came the young witch, with her red hair flowing in the wind. She wore a dress of gold tissue decorated with peacocks' eyes, and a little cap of green velvet was on her head.

She ran to the hornbeam, and taking the Fisherman by the hand she led him out into the moonlight and began to dance.

Round and round they whirled. And while they danced, they heard the galloping of a horse, although no horse was visible. The Fisherman was scared, but the witch said, 'faster', and they twirled even faster, her arms around his neck. 'Faster! Faster!' the witch cried, and the earth seemed to spin beneath his feet, and a great terror fell on him. Eventually, he became aware of a figure that had not been there before.

It was a man dressed in a suit of black velvet. His face was pale, but his lips were like a proud red flower. He seemed weary, and was leaning back toying in a listless manner with the pommel of his dagger. On the grass beside him lay a plumed hat, and a pair of riding gloves covered with gilt lace, and sewn with seed-pearls shaped into a curious device. A short cloak lined with sables hung from his shoulder, and his delicate white hands were decorated with rings. Heavy eyelids hanged loosely over his eyes. The Fisherman watched him, as though spellbound. At last their eyes met, and the man's eyes seemed to follow him wherever he danced. He heard the witch laugh, and caught her by the waist, and whirled her madly round and round.

Suddenly a dog bayed, and the dancers stopped. Two by two, they knelt down, and kissed the man's hands. He smiled disdainfully as they did so, but kept looking at the Fisherman.

The young witch led him forward towards the man, and he followed. However, when he came close, and without knowing why he did it, he made the sign of the Cross, and called upon the holy name.

As soon as he did that, the witches screamed like hawks and flew away, and man's face twitched in pain. The man whistled, and a horse came running to meet him. As he leapt into the saddle, he turned round and looked at the Fisherman sadly.

The red-haired witch tried to fly away also, but the Fisherman caught her by her wrists.

'Let me go,' she cried, 'you have named what should not be named, and shown the sign that may not be looked at.'

'No,' he answered, 'I will not let you go until you have told me the secret.'

She begged him to ask her anything but that, and he threatened to kill her if she did not keep her promise.

'Alright then, it's your soul! Do what you will,' she said, and gave him a little knife with a handle of green viper's skin.

'What is this?' he asked.

'Your shadow is not your body's shadow; it is the body of your soul. Cut it free and send it away if that is what you really want to do.'

'Is this true?' he murmured.

She nodded and told him how to do it.

***

As he came down the mountain, the Fisherman's soul called out to him.

It said, 'Lo! I have lived with you all these years, and have been your servant. Do not send me away! When have I ever wronged you?'

And the Fisherman laughed.

'You have not wronged me, but I do not need you,' he answered. 'The world is wide; go wherever you will, but leave me alone, for my love is calling me.'

His soul begged and begged, but he ignored it, until he finally reached the seashore. There, he stood with his back to the moon, as the witch had told him to. Before him lay his shadow—the body of his Soul—and behind him, the moon hung in the honey-coloured air.

Eventually, his Soul said, 'If you really want me to go, at least give me your heart, for the world is a cruel place.'

The Fisherman laughed.

'What would I give my love if I gave you my heart?' he cried, refusing his Soul's request.

Then the Fisherman took the little knife and cut away the shadow from around his feet. Then, he tried to chase his Soul away. However, it insisted that they should meet once a year.

'You might need me,' it said. When it spoke, the Soul's voice was low and flute-like.

'Do as you like,' the Fisherman said, and dived into the water, to be with his mermaid, who rose up to greet him.

And the Soul stood on the lonely beach and watched them. And when they had sunk down into the sea, it went away, weeping.

After a year was over, the Soul came back to the seashore and called to the Fisherman.

'Come near,' it said, 'so I can tell you of the marvellous things I have seen!'

So he came nearer, and couched in the shallow water, and leaned his head upon his hand and listened.

The Soul told the Fisherman that, after it had left him, it journeyed East and, after many adventures, had found the Mirror of Wisdom.

'And I did a strange thing, but what I did does not matter, for in a valley that is but a day's journey here, I have hidden the Mirror of Wisdom. Let me join you again, and you shall be wiser than all the wise men. Come with me, and wisdom shall be yours.'

However, the Fisherman laughed.

'Love is better than wisdom,' he cried, 'and the little mermaid loves me.'

Then he dove back into the sea; the Soul stood on the lonely beach and went away weeping.

***

After the second year was over, the Soul came back to the seashore and called to the Fisherman.

'Come near,' it said, 'so I can tell you of the marvellous things I have seen!'

So he came nearer, and couched in the shallow water, and leaned his head upon his hand and listened.

'After I left you, I travelled South, where all the world's treasures come from. There, I met a prince, who tried to kill me for not bowing to him. When he could not kill me, he offered me half of the great riches that his kingdom owned. I refused, and asked, instead, for the little lead ring that he wore on his little finger. Then, he offered me all the riches in his kingdom, but I refused, for I knew that the ring was not any ordinary ring. It was the Ring of Riches.'

It continued, 'And I did a strange thing, but what I did does not matter, for in a valley that is but a day's journey here, I have hidden the Ring of Riches. Let me join you again, and you shall be richer than all the kings of the world. Come, take it and all the world's riches shall be yours.'

However, the Fisherman laughed.

'Love is better than riches,' he cried, 'and the little mermaid loves me.'

Then he dove back into the sea; the Soul stood on the lonely beach and went away weeping.

After the third year was over, the Soul came back to the seashore and called to the Fisherman.

'Come near,' it said, 'so I can tell you of the marvellous things I have seen!'

So he came nearer, and couched in the shallow water, and leaned his head upon his hand and listened.

And the Soul said to him, 'I know a city not far from here, where there is an inn near a river. There I saw a girl dance: Her face was covered with a veil of transparent fabric, but her feet were naked. And her naked feet moved over the carpet like little white pigeons. Never have I seen anything so marvellous!'

These words reminded the Fisherman that the little mermaid had no feet and could not dance. Suddenly, he longed to watch someone dance.

He said to himself, 'It is just a day's journey, and I can return to my love,' and he laughed, and stood up in the shallow water, and strode towards the shore.

And when he had reached the dry shore, he laughed again, and held out his arms to his Soul. And his Soul gave a great cry of joy and ran to meet him, and the Fisherman saw his shadow—the body of the Soul—stretching before him once more.

And his Soul said to him, 'Come on, let's leave at once for the sea gods are jealous and can send monsters out to attack us!'

The Fisherman and his Soul hurried away. They travelled the whole night and the whole day, and finally came upon a city the next evening.

And the Fisherman said to his Soul, 'Is this the city where the girl dances with naked feet?'

And his Soul replied, 'No, not this city, but we should enter anyway.'

So they entered the city, where the Soul told the Fisherman to steal a silver cup that was on display in a shop window. He hid it among his clothes and they hurried out of the city.

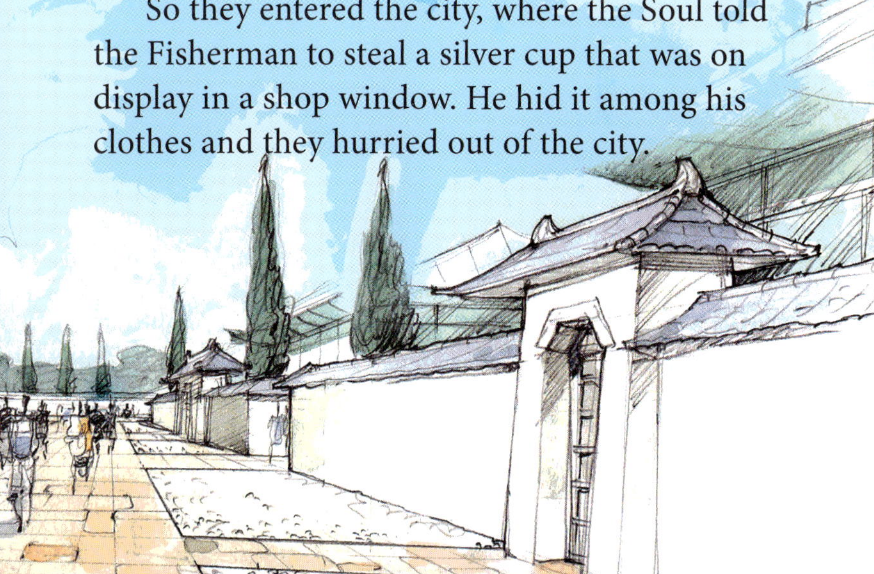

Once they had gone some distance, the Fisherman frowned, and threw the cup away, and said to his Soul, 'Why did you tell me to steal this cup and hide it? That was an evil thing to do.'

But his Soul answered, 'Be at peace, be at peace.'

On the evening of the second day, they came to another city.

Again, the Fisherman asked his Soul, 'Is this the city where the girl dances with naked feet?'

And his Soul replied, 'No, not this city, but we should enter anyway.'

Here, the Soul told the Fisherman to beat a child. And the Fisherman beat the child till he cried. Then they hurried away.

Once they had gone some distance, the Fisherman got angry and said to his Soul, 'Why did you tell me to beat that child? That was an evil thing to do.'

But his Soul answered, 'Be at peace, be at peace.'

On the third evening, they came to another city.

Again, the Fisherman asked his Soul, 'Is this the city where the girl dances with naked feet?'

And his Soul replied, 'This might be the city. Let us enter.'

They entered the city, but could not find the inn that stood near the river. The Fisherman became uneasy with the looks people were giving him, so he suggested that they leave. However, the Soul replied that it was dark and there might be robbers around. So they sat down in the market and rested, and after a while, a hooded merchant addressed them.

'Why are you sitting in the market, even when all the stalls and shops are closed?'

And the Fisherman answered, 'I can find no inn in this city, nor do I have any relatives here.'

At this, the merchant invited the Fisherman—and his Soul—to spend the night at his house. There, the merchant treated him like an honoured guest and, after he had eaten, led him to the guest bedroom. The Fisherman thanked him and quickly fell asleep.

About three hours before dawn, the Fisherman's Soul woke him up and said, 'Go to merchant's bedroom, kill him, and take his gold. We will need all of it.'

As usual, the Fisherman followed his Soul's orders.

Once they had gone some distance, the Fisherman began to feel sad, and said to his Soul, 'Why did you make me kill the merchant and take his gold? Surely, you are evil!'

But his Soul answered, 'Be at peace, be at peace.'

'No!' cried the Fisherman, 'I cannot be at peace, for you have made me do everything I hate! I hate you also, and I demand to know why you have brought me like this!'

His Soul answered, 'When you sent me away, I begged you for a heart, but you did not give it. So I learnt to do all these "evil" things, and I love them. But be at peace, for you shall not feel any pain, and there shall be no pleasures that you will not receive.'

The Fisherman trembled when he heard these words.

He said to his Soul, 'You are evil! You have made me forget my love, and you have tempted me and led me into sin.'

The Soul then tried to coax the Fisherman into continuing on their journey, but the Fisherman refused. He drew out the little knife and fell onto one knee, ready to cut away his Soul again. Nothing happened. His Soul remained attached to him.

The Fisherman's Soul then laughed and said that the witch's spell would not work anymore, since a man could only send his Soul away once in a lifetime; once he had received it back, it would never leave him again.

'This is his punishment and his reward.'

When the Fisherman realized he could no longer get rid of his evil Soul, he fell upon the ground weeping bitterly.

The next morning, the Fisherman told his Soul, 'I will tie up my hands so that they do not do your bidding and close my lips so I don't speak your words. And I will return to the little bay where my love likes to sing, and I will call to her and tell her the evil that you have made me do.'

In response, his Soul tempted him and said, 'Who is your love that you should return to her? The world has many fairer than she is. There are the dancing girls of Samaris, whose feet are painted with henna, and in their hands they have little copper bells. They laugh while they dance, and their laughter is as clear as the laughter of water. Come with me and I will show them to you. Why are you so concerned about sin? Come with me, and I will show you a garden of tulips, where peacocks roam. She who feeds them dances for them. Her eyes are darkened with kohl, and in one of her nostrils she wears a flower that is carved out of pearl. She laughs while she dances, and her silver anklets tinkle. And stop worrying, and come with me to this city.'

However, the Fisherman did not answer his Soul. He tied his hands tight with cord, sealed his lips and—ignoring his Soul's constant attempts to tempt him—returned to the bay where his love liked to sing.

And when he had reached the shore of the sea, he loosened the cord from his hands, unsealed his lips and called to the little mermaid. But she did not come; even though he called to her all day long.

And his Soul laughed at him, saying, 'You are like one who pours water into a broken pot in the middle of a drought. You pour everything into your love, but get nothing in return. Come with me, and I will take you to the Valley of Pleasure, where you will want for nothing.'

The Fisherman did not respond, but built himself a house in a cleft in the rock. He lived there for a year, and called to her three times every day—in the morning, at noon, and at night—but she never came. Neither could he find her in the caves, nor in the deep waters nor in the pools of the tide and in the wells that are at the bottom of the deep.

Through the year, his Soul kept tempting him, but his love was so strong that he prevailed against its unpleasant whisperings.

When the year was over, the Soul thought to itself, 'I have tempted my master with evil, but his love is stronger than I am. I will tempt him now with good; maybe he will come with me then.'

So he said, 'I have told you of the joys of the world, and you have ignored me. I will now tell you of the world's pain; maybe you will listen then. For truly, there is no one who escapes from its net. There are some who lack clothes, and others who lack food. There are widows who sit in purple, and widows who sit in rags, and they are cruel to each other. The beggars go up and down on the highways, and their wallets are empty. Through the streets of the cities walks famine, and the plague sits at their gates. Come, let us go forth and mend these things. Why should you waste time here, when she does not answer your call?'

But the Fisherman did not answer, so great was the power of his love. And he called to her three times every day—in the morning, at noon, and at night—but she never came. Neither could he find her in the caves, nor in the deep waters nor in the pools of the tide and in the wells that are at the bottom of the deep.

When the second year was over, the Soul said to the Fisherman, 'I have tempted you with evil, and I have tempted you with good, but your love is stronger than I am. Therefore, I will not tempt you any longer, but I beg you to allow me to enter your heart so I may be a part of you again.'

The Fisherman gave his leave, but his heart was so full of love for the little mermaid that there was no place in it for his Soul.

Just then, a great cry went up from the ocean—the cry that men hear when one of the sea folk is dead. The Fisherman jumped up when he heard this and rushed to the shore, where he saw the dead body of the little mermaid floating on the water. White as the surf it was, and like a flower it tossed on the waves. And the surf took it from the waves, and the foam took it from the surf, and the shore received it. Soon, it lay at his feet.

He flung himself down beside the little mermaid, weeping. Her red lips were cold, yet he kissed them. Her hair was salty, yet he tasted it with a bitter joy. He kissed the closed eyelids, and the wild spray that lay upon their cups was less salty than his tears.

And to the dead mermaid he made his confession. Into the shells of her ears he poured his tale. He put her little hands round his neck, and with his fingers he touched the thin reed of her throat. Bitter, bitter was his joy, and full of strange gladness was his pain.

So great was his pain, and his joy, that he did not see the black sea come nearer, or hear the white foam moan like a leper. With white claws of foam the sea grabbled at the shore. From the palace of the sea king came the cry of grief again, and far out upon the sea the sea folk blew hoarsely upon their horns.

'Flee!' his Soul said, 'for the sea comes ever closer; it will kill you if you stay here! Flee, for I am afraid, and your heart is closed to me because of the greatness of your love. Flee to a safe place! Surely you will not send me into another world without a heart?'

The Fisherman did not listen to his Soul, but called on the little mermaid and said, 'Love is better than wisdom, and more precious than riches, and fairer than the feet of the daughters of men. The fires cannot destroy it, nor can the waters satisfy it. I called on you at dawn, but you did not come. The moon heard your name, yet you did not heed me. For evilly had I left you, and had wandered away, to my own pain. Yet my love for you was strong. And now that you are dead, surely I will die with you also.'

And his Soul begged him to leave, but he would not, so great was his love. As the sea came nearer and nearer, the Fisherman's heart finally broke and his Soul found a space in it again. Eventually, the sea covered the Fisherman with its waves.

The next morning, the priest went forth to bless the sea, for it had been troubled. With him, went monks and musicians and candle bearers, swingers of censers, and a great crowd.

When the priest reached the shore, he saw the Fisherman lying drowned in the surf, and clasped in his arms was the body of the little mermaid.

And he drew back frowning, and having made the sign of the Cross, he cried aloud and said, 'I will not bless the sea nor anything that is in it. Cursed be the sea folk, and cursed be all they who are involved with them. And as for him who forsook God for love's sake, and so lies here with his lover slain by God's judgment, take up his body and the body of his lover, and bury them in the corner of the Field of the Fullers, and set no mark above them, nor any kind of sign, that no one may know their resting place. For cursed were they in their lives, and cursed shall they be in their deaths also.'

The people did as he told them, and in the corner of the Fullers' Field, they dug a deep pit, where no sweet herbs grew, and laid the dead things within it.

Soon, three years went by, and on one holy day, the priest went up to the chapel.

When he entered the chapel and bowed before the altar, he saw that the altar was covered with strange flowers that he had never seen before. They smelled sweet and were strangely beautiful; and their beauty troubled him. He was glad, but did not understand why.

The priest had intended to show people the wounds of the Lord and preach a sermon on the wrath of God. However, when he began to speak, his words were not of God's anger but of the God whose name is Love. And he did not know why it was so.

When he had finished, the people wept; even the priest's eyes were full of tears.

After the service, he asked one of his helpers, 'What are the flowers that stand on the altar, and where do they come from?'

No one knew what flowers they were, but they told him they grew in the corner of the Fullers's Field. On hearing this, the priest trembled, and returned to his own house and prayed.

And in the morning, while it was still dawn, he went forth with the followers and blessed the sea, and all the wild things in it. Then, he blessed the woodland as well, and all the little things that dance there. All the things in God's world he blessed, and the people were filled with joy and wonder.

Never again did the flowers grow in the corner of the Fullers' Field, and it returned to its original barren state. Nor came the sea folk into the bay as they used to, for they went to another part of the sea.

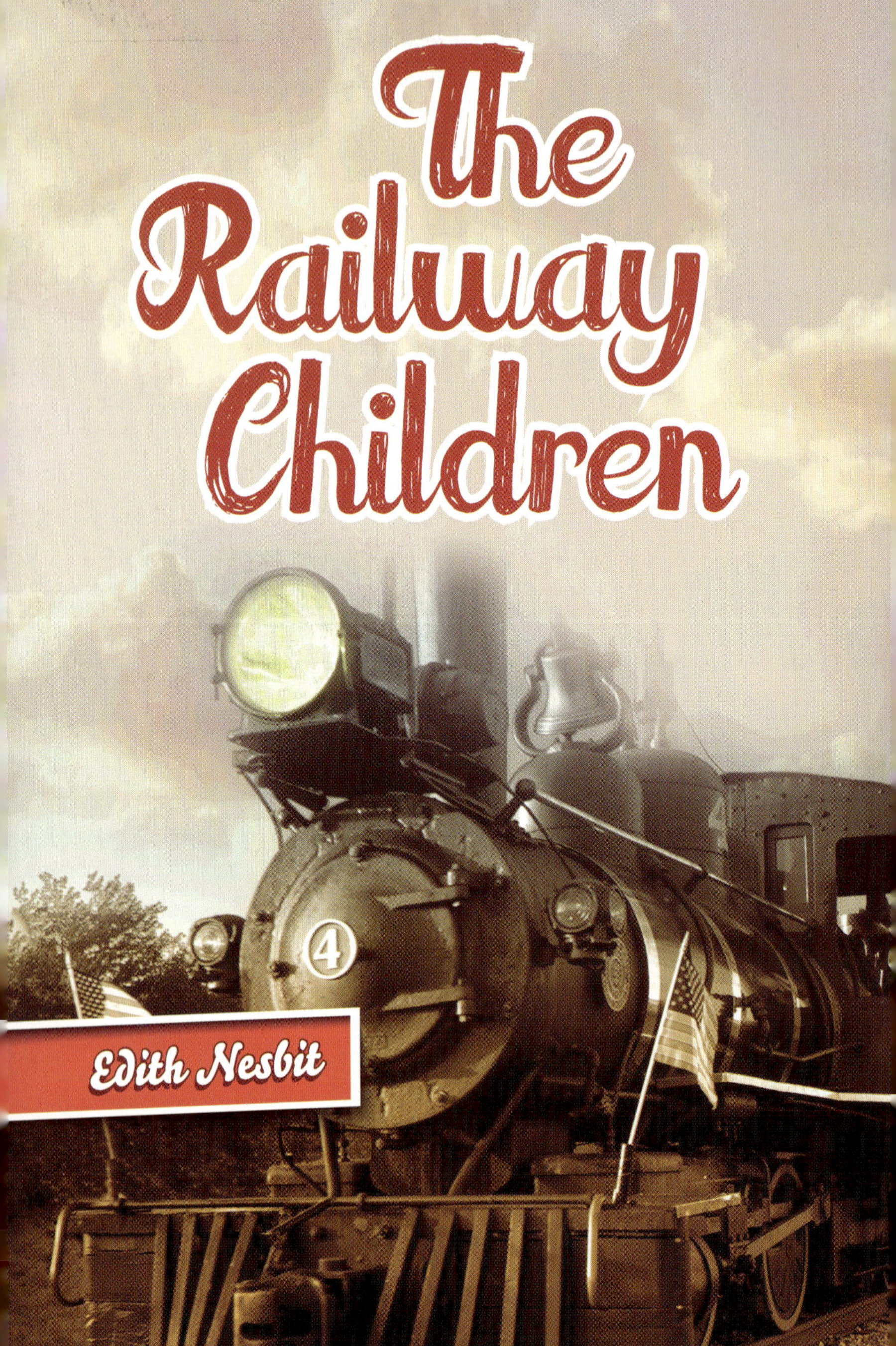

The Railway Children
Edith Nesbit

For a long while, Roberta (Bobbie), Peter and Phyllis were simple, suburban children. Mother was always ready to play games with them, read to them, and help them with their homework. She also wrote stories and composed funny poems for different occasions. Father never got angry, was never unjust and ready at most times for a game. The children in short, had everything they wanted.

But a dreadful change happened rather suddenly.

Three days after Peter's tenth birthday, his new model engine stopped working suddenly. Of all the gifts he had received, this had been his favourite. Peter was very upset, but waited patiently for Father to return from his trip out of town. When Father did come back, he looked the engine over carefully, and cheerfully announced that he would fix it that weekend.

Suddenly there was a knock at the front door.

Two gentlemen wanted to meet the master of the house. So Father took them into his study. After a while, Mother went to the library. The children heard much talking. Ruth, the maid, ordered a cab. After a while, the cab drove off with the men and Father.

When Mother came back, looking pale as ever, she simply told Ruth, 'Ruth, get everyone into bed!'

In the morning, the children's mother left for London.

'Something awful has happened', said Peter at breakfast. The others agreed, but no one knew what it was.

Mother returned at seven that evening, looking tired and ill. The children did not ask any questions.

Finally, Mother said, 'My darlings! The men who came here brought bad news. Father will be away for a while.'

Roberta asked, 'Father worked in a government office; is that the trouble?'

Mother replied, 'Yes. Now off to bed all of you!'

***

A few days later, Mother announced to her children, 'My dears, we're moving to the country, where we'll live in a lovely little house. You'll love it!'

The next week was spent in packing—clothes, tables, chairs and other household goods. Soon, everything was sent to the new house, a taxi took the family to the station. Soon, they were dropped off on a cold and gloomy platform in the countryside.

As the train left, the children saw its tail-lights fade into the darkness. Little did they know how important this platform, and trains, would become to them!

There were no cabs, so they walked behind the cart that carried their goods.

After a while Mother said, 'There's our new house.' She was pointing to a dark house.

'I don't know why the woman I hired has closed the shutters,' she added.

There was a garden, which, Peter said, 'Looks like a pan dripping with black cabbages!'

The man who drove the cart said, 'Mrs Viney may have gone home, for your train was very late.'

'The key will be under the steps,' he added.

They found it and opened the door.

The curtains and hearth rug were missing while the chairs lay in one corner and the pans, pots, crockery and brooms in another. More importantly, the kitchen was bare.

Mother was confused.

'But I'd asked Mrs Viney to keep meat, bread, butter, and other foodstuff for us,' she said.

They searched all the rooms, but found nothing to eat!

So they went to the cellar where all their things were stored, opened a few of the cases and found candles and an odd combination of tinned food left over from the old pantry. That night, Mother and the children ate biscuits, sardines, preserved ginger, candied peel, cooking raisins and marmalade. They drank a toast with water using tea cups.

Luckily, they found sheets. And, since the men who had shifted the furniture had put the beds together, they had a cosy place to sleep!

Next morning, the children woke up very early, and decided to explore their neighbourhood. The land was hilly, so they could look down on a railway line and the gaping, black opening of a tunnel. They could not see the railway station, but they saw a big bridge running across the valley.

Peter said, 'Let's go look at the station!'

'We'll see it from here,' said Roberta. 'Let's sit down for a while.'

They sat down on a big flat stone and were soon fast asleep.

At eight o'clock, Mother woke them up, saying, 'Come quickly! I've found a magic room!'

When Mother opened the door, they saw, laid out neatly on the table: roast beef, bread, butter, a pie and cheese—the previous night's dinner! They had mistaken the door to the dining room for a cupboard the previous night!

After breakfast, Bobbie, Peter and Phyllis visited the railway station.

'What is that white mark on the wall near the coal?' Peter asked the porter who was lounging nearby.

The porter, whose name was Perks, answered, 'The line marks the level of coal, so you know if any of it gets stolen.'

***

June was wet. The children wanted to light a fire, but Mother said they couldn't, since coal was very expensive.

'Romp about in the attic,' she said, 'it will warm you up.'

Peter had an idea. He told his siblings to bring the 'Roman Chariot'—an old perambulator—and trudged along to the coal heap near the railway station.

'St Peter's coal mine,' he announced. 'We'll haul some home in our chariot.'

Mother's coal cellar was soon quite full!

A week later, Mrs Viney wondered at how long their coal was lasting.

Then, one night, the Station Master caught Peter—with a bag full of the precious fuel.

'I'm not a robber,' Peter said, 'I'm a coal miner.'

'Tell your yarn to the Marines,' the Station Master retorted.

Peter was in trouble! Luckily for the children, however, the Station Master let them all go with a stern warning.

'Robbing is robbing,' he said, 'even if you call it "mining".'

***

Despite this 'setback', the children could not stay away from the railway station. The passing trains linked the children's lives to the one they had earlier.

One day, Phyllis said, 'Let's wave together to the *Green Dragon* when it passes. If it's a magic train, it'll carry our love to Father.'

When this particular train roared into the station, the three children waved their handkerchiefs. Out of a carriage a hand waved at them! It was a white-haired old gentleman, who they had regularly seen on this train. He was good-looking and wore funny-shaped collars and a hat that was different from what others wore!

Thereafter, they exchanged waves with the 9:15 *Green Dragon* every day.

Mother, meanwhile, wrote a lot and sent her stories to publishers.

Sometimes, when an editor accepted one of her stories, she would celebrate and they would all have buns for tea.

But, one day, Mother's head ached and she was burning hot. She could not eat and her throat was quite sore. On Mrs Viney's advice, Bobbie ran to fetch Dr W. W. Forest. He diagnosed Mother's illness as influenza.

'I'll send some medicine. Keep the fire going! Get her some brandy.'

When the 9:15 chugged into the station that morning, the old gentleman looked for the children, but saw only Peter. He was pointing to a big white sheet that was nailed onto the fence. On it was written: LOOK OUT AT THE STATION.

The train was pulling out of the station when the old gentleman saw Phyllis running towards him.

She said, 'Take this,' and pushed a warm, damp letter into his hand.

The man read the letter:

'Dear Mr… We don't know what your name is. Our mother is sick and the doctor says we must give her the items that are listed at the end of this letter. Father is away; when he returns he will pay you. Sined Peter.'

***

That evening, a knock was heard at the back door. The children rushed there and found the friendly porter standing with a big parcel in his hand.

'The old gentleman told me to give it to you,' he said.

'GP' something was signed at the bottom of the letter that came with the hamper.

The children then displayed another banner at the station. It read: SHE IS ALMOST WELL. THANK YOU.

When Mother found out about this, she told her children, as the tears poured from her eyes, 'We may be poor, but we got enough. Never ask strangers for things. Will you remember that?'

The children hugged their mother and promised her that they would remember.

***

The next day, Bobbie decided to mend Peter's engine secretly. She got the chance the next afternoon. The four of them were leaving to go to town, when Bobbie accidentally tore her dress. Mother was late, so she could not wait for Bobbie to change. So Bobbie was left to follow her own plans.

She wrapped the toy engine in some brown paper and carried it to the railway station. She had decided to ask an 'Engineer' to fix it.

When a train arrived, Bobbie found that the driver could not hear her call out. So she climbed into the engine and pulled at the engine driver's

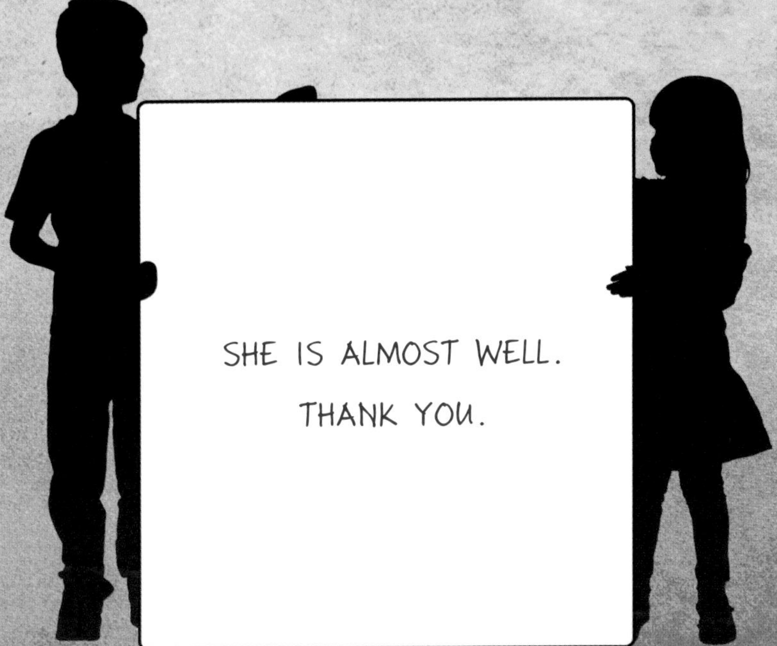

coats. However, by the time she climbed aboard, the train had begun to move!

Bobbie was scared. She clutched the sleeve nearest to her. The man whose sleeve it was, was startled. Bobbie and he stared at each other for some time.

Roberta started crying when the man called her mischievous. However, the driver and the fireman allowed her to sit on a seat and told her not to cry.

When she stopped crying, Bobbie showed them the broken engine, and said, 'I wanted to ask you if you'd mend this engine.'

The fireman was stunned, but he and the driver both looked at the toy engine.

At the next station, they handed Bobbie to the guard of another train, who brought her back safely.

The driver got his cousin to fix the toy engine and gave it to Bobbie the next time he came to 'her' station. It was now as good as new!

***

One morning, there was a commotion at the station. A crowd had gathered around a rather dishevelled stranger. He spoke a foreign language, had no ticket and did not seem to know where he was going. He also looked quite ill.

The children deciphered that the man was speaking French. All three had been taught

French at school. Now, they deeply wished that they had learned it!

Mother did speak fluent French, but had gone on a short trip to the nearby town. So, Phyllis asked the station master—who had announced that he would 'see to this'—to wait for her.

In the meantime, Peter showed the stranger some foreign stamps and the man reacted on seeing a Russian one.

Peter said, 'He's Russian!'

Soon Mother's train rolled in.

She said, 'He's definitely a Russian. He has lost his ticket, and he's quite ill. I'll take him home.'

Mother sent Bobbie for the doctor.

When the doctor came, the Russian was seated in Father's arm chair.

'The man is worn out, body and mind,' was the doctor's diagnosis. 'Put him to bed give him some warmth.'

Later, Mother told them, 'This man was a great writer. But he had to escape his country for the Czar did not like what he wrote. Friends got a message to him telling him that his children and wife had escaped to England. So he came here. He doesn't know where they are. I hope he finds them.'

***

The Russian was in better shape the next day and kept on getting better. Meanwhile, Mother wrote some letters to persons she felt could know the whereabouts of the Russian's family—strange people like paper editors, Members of Parliament and Society Secretaries.

One day, the children were walking towards the train tracks, where they were to have a picnic, when Bobbie suddenly stopped.

'What's that sound?' she asked.

It was a soft noise but it could be clearly heard. Then suddenly they saw a tree move and then more and more trees started to move!

Soon stones and pieces of earth fell and landed on the rail tracks below. It was a landslide.

Peter said, 'The 11:29 train has not passed by yet. There will be a terrible accident if we don't warn them!'

But there was no time to run to the station! So Bobbie and Phyllis gave Peter their red petticoats. Peter tore them into six pieces and tied them to pieces of wood which he cut from the trees. Then, they carried their 'flags' to the tracks and waited. It seemed like hours before they heard the train coming. Soon, they could see white steam puffing out the train!

Peter said, 'Everyone, wave like crazy and don't stop!'

The train was moving very fast. The children kept on waving their red 'flags'.

Nobody in the train seemed to have noticed them. Then Bobbie went on the track and planted two flags there. The train slowed down and came to a stop—some twenty yards away from Bobbie's flags.

She saw the engine halt but she could not stop waving. When the fireman and the driver stepped down from the train, Bobbie was still waving the flags.

She suddenly slumped and fell across the tracks! The driver lifted her and laid her down on a cushion-covered first class compartment.

Before they reached the station Bobbie regained consciousness. The others cheered loudly!

The railway authorities and passengers praised on the children for their prompt action and ingenuity.

As they left, Phyllis said, 'How lucky that we wore our red coloured petticoats!'

***

The Russian was on everybody's minds. People replied to Mother's letters politely, but no one could any information about Mr Szezcpansky's wife and kids. (Incidentally, the Russian's name was Szezcpansky.)

Bobbie tried her best to please him but she didn't get much success. But his presence made Mother happy.

One day, the children received a letter. It read:

Dear Ladies and Sir,

We wish to present you gifts, in commemoration of your courageous and prompt action in averting what would have been a horrible accident. The presentation ceremony will take place at the station at three o'clock on the 30th.

It was signed by the secretary of the Railway Company.

It was proudest moment in the children's lives! They rushed with the letter to Mother, who was also very proud.

'If they give money it would be better not to take it,' said Mother.

The children then replied to the letter from the Railway, saying that the place and time would suit them well.

At the presentation, the children's names were called one by one, and each of them received a gold watch on a lovely chain. Their names were engraved on the watches. The children thanked everyone properly.

Back home, Bobbie penned a letter to the old gentleman. It ran: 'Mother says we must not ask for and take things from others. We just want to speak to you about a Captive and Prisoner. Your loving friend, Bobbie.'

***

The children met the old gentleman and Bobbie related to him the Russian's story.

'We want you to help find his wife and children,' she said.

The gentleman opened a page in his note book and told Bobbie to write his name there.

She wrote, 'Szezcpansky.'

When the gentleman saw the name, he said, 'I've read his book; it has been translated into all European languages. It's a noble book! Every Russian in England will know this name!'

He then asked the children to tell him everything about themselves. And they did that, not missing out any detail.

***

Some days went by and they got a visitor. It was the old gentleman, his brass buttons shining in the sunshine, his waistcoat looking even whiter in the backdrop of the green field.

'Hullo!' the children shouted and waved their hands.

He returned their 'Hullo!' and waved his hat.

'I've got good news for you,' he said. 'I've found the Russian writer's wife and child. I decided to come personally to give you the news.'

Bobbie ran in and breathlessly broke the news to her mother and the Russian.

The Russian jumped up, gave out a cry of pleasure and kissed Mother's hand. He then put his hands on his face and wept with joy!

The old gentleman joined them and asked Mother if he could give the children some 'goodies'. Mother gave him permission and the children's hands were soon full of chocolates!

***

One day, the children asked Perks, the porter, when his birthday was. 'I was born thirty-two years ago, on the 15th of this month,' he said.

'Will you be celebrating it?' Phyllis asked.

'No, I've got to look after my family,' he replied.

The children then decided to arrange something for Perks's birthday and went to the canal to discuss their plans.

It was getting dark, when Phyllis suddenly said, 'What is that?'

Smoke was coming out of the chimney of the cabin in which the bargeman lived with his wife and baby.

Bobbie screamed, 'The baby!'

All three dashed for the barge and they rowed it to the cabin.

Peter put his wet handkerchief on his mouth and Bobbie, saying 'let me go', rushed first into the cabin.

'I've got the baby,' Peter said and he staggered onto the deck.

Bobbie caught the dog.

They handled the baby with utmost care and Bobbie ran as fast as she could to the Rose and Crown, the place where bargees meet.

Bobbie ran in and said loudly, 'I'm looking for Bill the Bargeman. Your cabin is on fire.'

'My baby!' Bill's wife cried out.

'The baby's safe,' Bobbie reassured her, 'so is the dog.'

Bill and his wife were overjoyed that the children had done them such a good service.

Bill told them, 'Come here tomorrow at seven. I will take you all for a long trip to Farley. All for free!'

They were there the next morning, with soda cake, bread, cheese and some mutton in a basket.

They had a glorious day!

***

Mother announced, 'I've sold one more story! So you'll get buns with tea.'

The children looked at each other.

Bobbie said, 'Mother, can we have the buns on the 15th?'

'You can have buns whenever you like, dear,' Mother said. 'Why 15th?'

'Perks's birthday is on that day. He says he has stopped celebrating his birthday because he has to first take care of his wife and children.'

Peter added, 'We feel we can make it a wonderful birthday for him. He's been very decent to us, Mother.'

Peter got an idea.

'Perks has been good to everyone in the village. Let's ask them to chip in for the celebrations,' he said.

The children found that it wasn't easy to get people to think like them. Some people agreed to the proposal, some didn't.

The next morning Bobbie and Phyllis put a large bouquet of roses in a basket, along with needle book and gave it to old Mrs Ransome, who worked at the post office. The day before, she had abruptly told them that today was her birthday but no one was celebrating it for her!

On the 15th Mother made the buns with 'AP'—Perks' initials—written on them with pink sugar. On the way to Perks's house, they met Mrs Ransome. She gave them a basket—full of red, juicy gooseberries.

Mrs Ransome also had with her a pram for the Perks. She said it had belonged to her grand-daughter, who had died many years ago.

They packed all Perks's gifts in the perambulator and wheeled it to his small, yellow house.

When Mrs Perks saw the gifts, she burst out crying.

'These are tears of joy,' she said. 'Perks never had a birthday like this!'

***

Bobbie was carrying a parcel one day and as she had to wait at the railway crossing while the train passed by, she put the parcel on the gate. She casually started to read the paper with which the parcel was packed.

All of a sudden she clutched onto the parcel and read the paper again. It was like a horrible dream! She kept on reading, but the bottom half of the news column was cut off.

She somehow got home and tiptoed her way to her room and shut the door. She untied the parcel and read the column again. Her feet and hands turned icy cold; her face began to burn.

The newspaper headlines read: 'Trial Ends. Verdict. Sentence.'

'Now I know,' she told herself.

Father had been on trial, found guilty and sentenced to five years in prison!

'Oh, Father,' she said and crushed the paper. 'It isn't true. I know you didn't do it!'

***

Tea wasn't a happy meal. Bobbie looked ill but she didn't want to reveal her secret in front of Peter and Phyllis. Phyllis thought Bobbie was sick and stroked her hand sympathetically. Bobbie thought the meal would never end. When Mother cleared the table, Bobbie went behind her.

'She's done something and has gone to confess to Mother,' Phyllis said to Peter.

Bobbie caught Mother's hand.

'What's the matter?' Mother asked.

Bobbie said, 'Come up with me.'

When they were alone, Bobbie closed the door and hugged her mother! She could find no words and only said, 'Oh, Mummy, Mummy,' repeatedly.

Then Bobbie pulled the paper out from where she had hidden it.

Mother cried, 'Do you believe it?

'No!' Bobbie answered, her voice almost a shout.

Mother said, 'It's untrue. He's an honourable and noble man. But they have imprisoned him.'

Bobbie clung to her mother, saying, 'Daddy, oh, Daddy!'

Mother said, 'Don't tell the others.'

She added, 'Father was charged with selling government secrets to Russia. They said he was a traitor, a spy! Somebody else did it and Father was blamed for it.'

One week later, when she was alone, Bobbie wrote a letter to the old gentleman.

It read:

'Dear friend. What you read in this newspaper is not true. Mother says that some person put the secret papers in Father's drawer in his office. Father suspected this person for a long time but nobody listened to him. Can you find the real traitor so that he can be freed?

Please help me.

Love, Roberta.'

She put the paper cutting with her letter in the envelope and gave it to the Station Master and asked him to deliver it to the gentleman.

***

One day, while the children were out, they saw a hare being chased by hounds—thirty in all.

Behind them ran a boy in a red jersey. The entire group entered the tunnel.

The children ran behind them, for they knew that the tunnel was not a really safe place, especially if you've not been there before.

It was a long time before the hare returned—followed soon by the hounds. But there was no sign of the boy in the red jersey.

'Let's eat, I'm very hungry,' said Bobbie and soon she and Phyllis had their mouths full.

Peter said, 'The red-jerseyed boy may have had an accident. A passing train…'

Bobbie said loudly, 'Come behind me.'

'A train's coming!' said Bobbie.

The roar of the train became louder. Peter shouted very loudly, Bobbie heard his call.

The train was near them. Soon, it zoomed past the children and, in a few seconds, all they could see were its tail-lights.

There started to explore the tunnel and before long saw the boy. His arms dangled by his sides. His eyes were closed.

***

They threw some of the milk from their picnic lunch onto his face, and the boy sighed.

'I'm better,' he announced. 'But I think my leg is broken,' he said. 'My name's Jim.'

Bobbie said, 'We'll take him home.'

When Jim was brought home, his face and body pale, Mother said, 'Good you brought him here.'

Jim saw kind eyes which comforted him.

'I hate to trouble you,' he said.

'Don't worry,' said Mother.

Peter said, 'We must send letters to his schoolmaster and grandfather.'

They heard someone come into the house. It was a familiar voice.

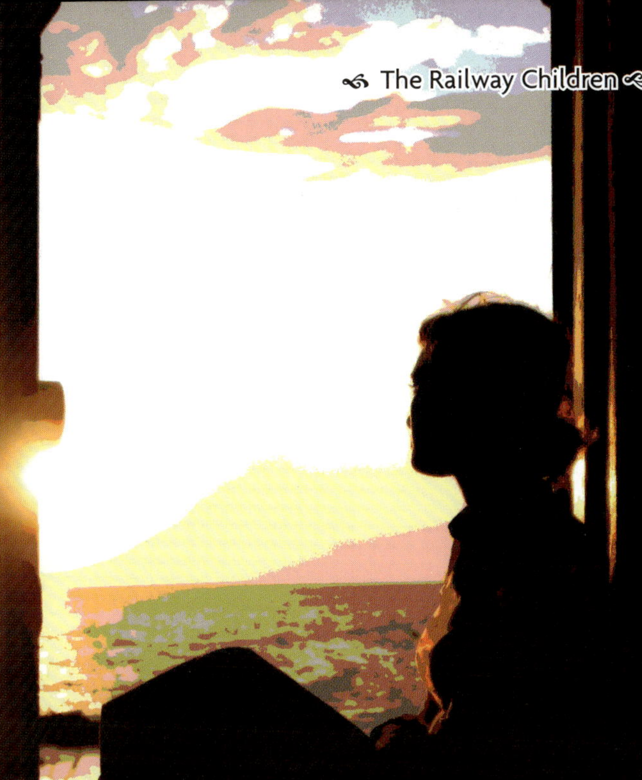

'It's Jim's grandfather,' Mother said. 'He wishes to see you!'

When the children entered the room, Mother was seated at the window and in Father's chair sat—the old gentleman!

'Well, I never!' said Peter. 'It's our old gentleman!' exclaimed Phyllis.

'It's you!' said Bobbie.

He said, 'Your Mother has agreed to stop her writing for some time and become Matron of Three Chimneys Hospital. My unfortunate Jim is the sole patient.'

'God bless Mother,' the old gentleman said and held both Mother's hands. 'Bobbie, come to the gate with me.'

At the gate he told Bobbie, 'I received your letter. From the start I had doubts about this case. I've have tried to get at the truth ever since I met you. I have great hopes, my dear!'

***

The next day, Bobbie decided to go to the station. On the way there, the post office lady kissed and hugged her; the draper's boy lifted his cap and said, 'Morning, Miss!' The blacksmith grinned broadly at her; the Station Master shook her hand vigorously and warmly and said, 'The 11:54's late, Miss.'

Bobbie knew something great was about to happen.

Perks told her, 'I read it in the paper!'

Bobbie stood alone with the Station Cat as the train roared in.

Three people stepped out—a countryman carrying two boxes of chickens; the grocer's wife, Miss Peckitt, and—

'Daddy! My Daddy!' Bobbie's scream brought hundreds of heads out of the train's windows.

They stared at a tall, pasty-faced man whose lips were set tight. A small girl was clinging onto him with her arms as well as legs; his arms held her tightly.

When they reached home, Father said, 'Go in Bobbie. Tell Mother everything's all right. The real culprit has been caught. Daddy has been freed.'

# Other Titles *in the* Series

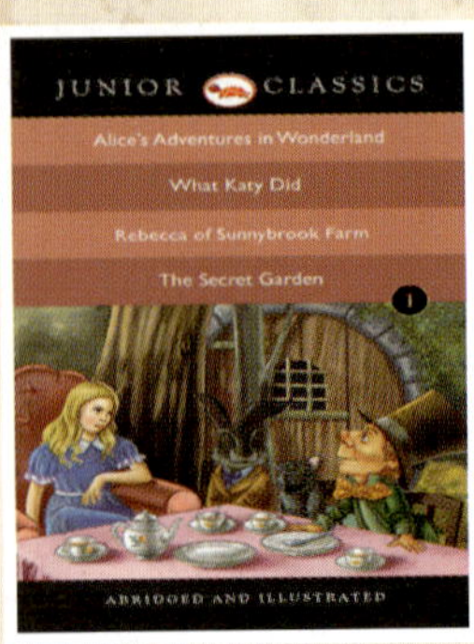

JUNIOR CLASSICS

Alice's Adventures in Wonderland

What Katy Did

Rebecca of Sunnybrook Farm

The Secret Garden

1

ABRIDGED AND ILLUSTRATED

JUNIOR CLASSICS

Captains Courageous

The Ingenious Gentleman Don Quixote of La Mancha

The Man in the Iron Mask

The Red Badge of Courage

2

ABRIDGED AND ILLUSTRATED

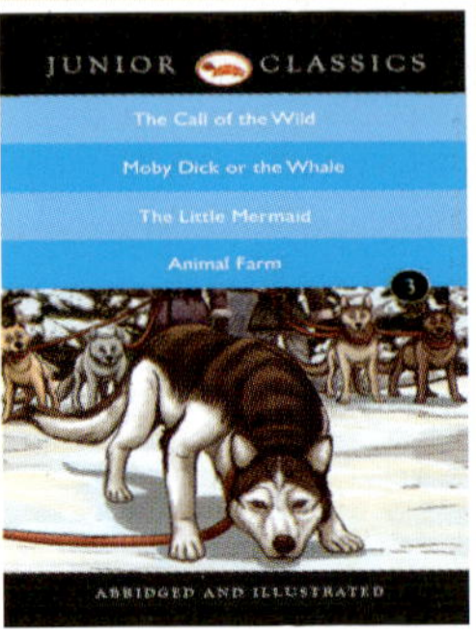

JUNIOR CLASSICS

The Call of the Wild

Moby Dick or the Whale

The Little Mermaid

Animal Farm

3

ABRIDGED AND ILLUSTRATED

JUNIOR CLASSICS

Heidi

A Tale of Two Cities

Little Women

Black Beauty

4

ABRIDGED AND ILLUSTRATED

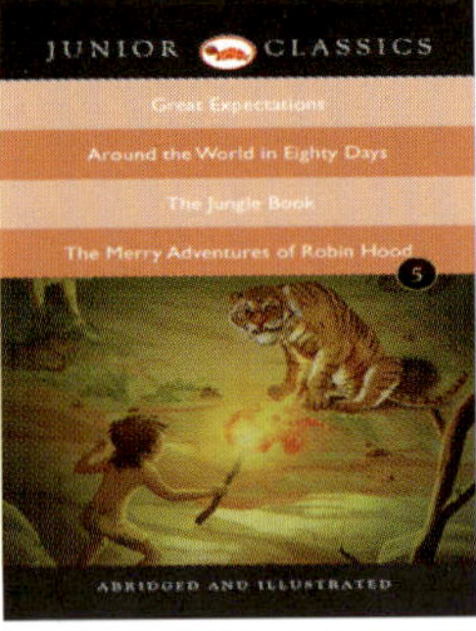

JUNIOR CLASSICS

Great Expectations

Around the World in Eighty Days

The Jungle Book

The Merry Adventures of Robin Hood

5

ABRIDGED AND ILLUSTRATED

JUNIOR CLASSICS

The Mutiny of the Bounty

The Adventures of Pinocchio

King Solomon's Mines

20,000 Leagues under the Sea

6

ABRIDGED AND ILLUSTRATED

JUNIOR CLASSICS

The Last of the Mohicans

The Legend of Sleepy Hollow

The Mayor of Casterbridge

The War of the Worlds

7

ABRIDGED AND ILLUSTRATED

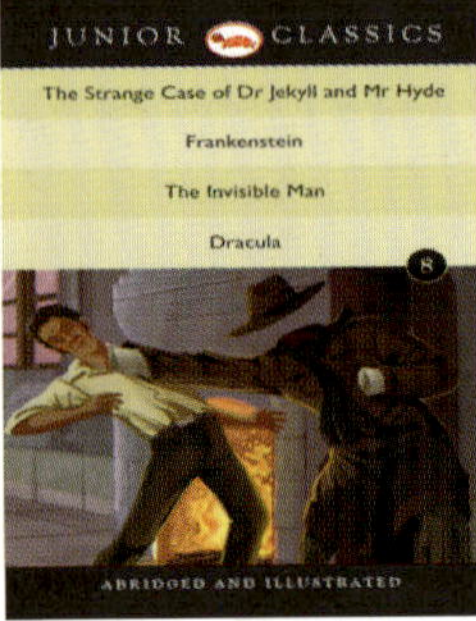

JUNIOR CLASSICS

The Strange Case of Dr Jekyll and Mr Hyde

Frankenstein

The Invisible Man

Dracula

8

ABRIDGED AND ILLUSTRATED

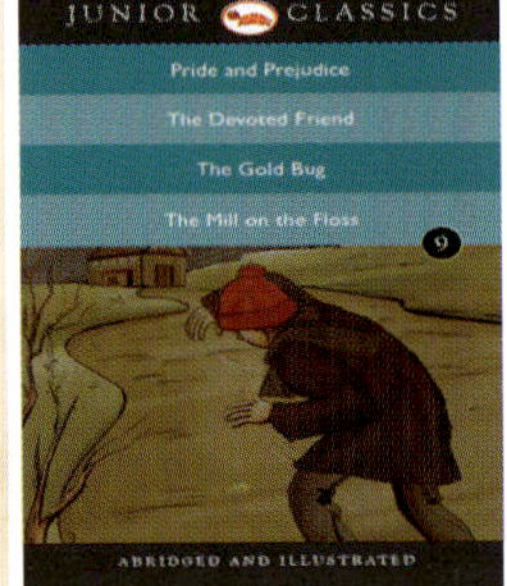

JUNIOR CLASSICS

Pride and Prejudice

The Devoted Friend

The Gold Bug

The Mill on the Floss

9

ABRIDGED AND ILLUSTRATED